MURDER AT THE
TOWN HALL

A ROSE BLAIR MURDER MYSTERY

JUDY KEIGHTLEY

Copyright © 2021 by Judy Keightley
Murder at the Town Hall
A Rose Blair Murder Mystery

ISBN-13: (Paperback) –978-0-9919187-2-0
Publisher: Judith Keightley

To Philip
My rock and foundation.

PROLOGUE

The Bayfield Town Hall was built in 1882 for the princely sum of $660. It was then moved to its present location on Clan Gregor Square in 1920. It was the seat of village government from that date until 1927, and again from 1965 to 1984.

When the village was unincorporated, the Town Hall continued in its use for community events.

Renovations were completed in 1981 with financial support from the Federal Government and the local community.

In 1983 the village established a Heritage Conservation District, which included the Town Hall. However, in 1984 the aging building had to be closed down as it failed to meet fire code standards at that time for community use.

In 1989 a committee was formed to restore the Town Hall, which by then had fallen into disrepair.

Many of the residents of Bayfield had fond memories of the Town Hall as the centre of village life and were reluctant to see it disappear.

The committee, then known as "The Friends of the Town Hall" re-energised community interest in the building and after several years of volunteer work, fundraising events, and private donations and grants, sufficient monies were raised to restore and maintain this historic building as a meeting and performance venue for the village.

The restoration maintained the integrity of the original 1882 structure, including keeping the former village jail which still remains, uninhabited, in the basement.

The Bayfield Town Hall Heritage Society is a now a non-profit corporation charged with the upkeep of this charming building.

There is a thriving Town Hall Committee who work very hard to make the hall an all-inclusive destination for concerts, weddings, plays, conferences, fitness programs, yoga, and many, many more events.

ONE

fterward, Rose could pinpoint the time when she knew, with certainty, that Tom was wavering in his love for her. She could see it in his eyes, his body language, and feel it in his touch. The biggest giveaway, however, was his reaction to Gillian Jeffries.

It was like an electric current had zapped through him when she walked in the room. His eyes lit up, his body straightened, and his whole demeanour softened taking years off his age. Rose hated Gillian Jeffries with a passion.

Tom and Rose had been having a quiet dinner at The Black Dog, a before the show repast. They had both ordered fish and chips and were just settling down to eat when Gillian walked in.

Taller and slimmer than Rose, Gillian wore her glossy chestnut coloured hair cascading down her back like a horse's mane. She wore a tight-fitting, low-necked sweater and equally slinky fitted black pants. There was a feline quality to her that instantly warned the females of the species to be on red alert.

Gillian had moved to Bayfield just over a year ago after a messy divorce from Andy Jeffries, an accountant from London. She had opened a fitness centre in the village called Time for Toning and it seemed that half of the men of Bayfield had taken out a membership, including Tom.

At first Rose had been amused at Tom's enthusiasm for fitness. After all, the only exercise that he had practised was in the summer when he played endless games of golf and sailed his boat. Rose had even encouraged and praised his dedication towards working out at the new gym. Every morning at 7:45 a.m., Tom would religiously jog over to the fitness centre. Gillian, the instructor, had told all her clients that if they lived within a 3km distance of Time for Toning she expected them to jog or at least walk as part of their fitness regime. Just like a puppy dog, Tom had obeyed his mistress, much to Rose's amusement.

IT WASN'T until three months into the program that Rose started to feel a little uncomfortable about Tom's dedication to fitness. She did, however, find out that some of her friends whose husbands had also enrolled into Time for Toning were beginning to feel irritated. Maybe they were all equally in Gillian's thrall and if that was the case, like all infatuations, it would fade, and no harm would be done.

It was February and the village was gripped in the middle of one of the fiercest winters that anyone had witnessed, at least in the past fifty years. Feet of snow covered the ground, and the trees were coated in what looked like pristine white cake icing dripping down in fingers of snow. Highway 21 had been closed several times already with freezing rain and white out conditions fit for the arctic.

There had been some concern over whether the band

that had been booked to play at the Town Hall would even make the drive from Toronto to Bayfield as the previous day had seen a dreadful blizzard and temperatures had plummeted to an all-time low of minus thirty-two. Rose, a new member of the Town Hall committee, had offered to put any of the band members up should they not want to drive back after the concert. She hadn't heard if her offer had been taken, but she had prepared the guest room just in case it was needed.

Tom and she were looking forward to the concert, as The Berries had been one of their favourite groups way back in the 70s. Joe Berry, the lead singer had been quite the dish in his day. Most of Rose's friends had a crush on him and if it hadn't been that Rose was madly in love with Tom at that time, she too would have joined the ranks of the smitten.

It was with a sigh of relief when word got out that the band had finally arrived in Bayfield and were currently eating dinner at The Albion. Rose looked at her watch and turned to Tom who was just finishing off his fish and chips.

"Tom, it's already seven o'clock. We should get going. The glasses have to be put out and I would like to be there to meet and greet the band. What was the name of the supporting group?"

TOM LOOKED THOUGHTFUL. "Well love, you should know as you're on the committee, but I do remember you telling me that they had booked a harpist called Cynthia for the supporting act. Do you know if she has arrived yet?"

"I don't know. I'll just phone Peggy as I'm sure that she'll know."

Rose pulled out her Samsung. Tom had given it to her the previous summer, and it had literally saved her life when she had been attacked on the beach. She now held the phone in great reverence and always promised Tom that she would leave it powered up and ready for emergencies.

Peggy answered the phone crisply. As Rose asked her question, she could just picture the chairwoman with her clip board crossing off the 'to-do' list. Peggy was a super-efficient and lovely woman and Rose held her in great esteem.

"Well Rose, no need to worry. I have Cynthia here at the Town Hall tuning up her harp as I speak. Everything's under control, although we are waiting for Tom to set out the bar and bring up the wine glasses."

Rose put her phone away and hurried Tom into finishing off his Guinness. As they left The Black Dog, she looked over her shoulder and caught Gillian Jeffries eye. She smiled sweetly at Rose and wiggled her fingers at Tom.

Tom had put his 'man-toy' sports car into storage for the winter. Rose had suggested that they walk to the pub from their house on Bayfield Terrace. As they left The Black Dog the chilling cold air numbed their faces. They trudged through the thick, dirty snow piled up on each side of the road. Rose held onto Tom's arm tightly. She did not want to fall and break her leg like her friend Wendy had four weeks ago. It had totally incapacitated her and made her house bound and reliant on her husband and friends.

They safely arrived at the Town Hall which looked particularly beautiful with its snow topped roof and twinkling outside lights. Rose immediately went upstairs to help with the collecting of tickets and Tom disappeared down- stairs to retrieve the glasses.

It was seven-fifteen, and The Berries were due to perform at about eight-thirty with Cynthia, the harpist, scheduled to play as an opener at eight p.m.

People started to trickle in soon after Rose and Tom had

arrived. There was still no sign of the band as yet, but Cynthia had come back down to the basement and was introduced to Rose by Peggy.

"Rose, meet Cynthia McArdle. She's from Halifax, Nova Scotia. Isn't that where your daughter Anne lives?"

At the mention of Anne, Rose's heart quickened. They were all on tenter hooks as the baby was due in the next week or two, the first week of March was the date that Anne had given her to keep free.

Anne, and her partner Alan, a Professor of Astrophysics at Dalhousie, seemed blissfully happy. The pregnancy had gone smoothly and now it was just a waiting game. Rose had of course promised to fly out to Halifax and help with the baby as soon as it was born. They had last seen their daughter the previous summer when she had first introduced them to Alan and then had proceeded to announce that they were expecting a baby.

That had all happened at the same time as when her good friend, Mary Stokes, had been murdered at the Croquet Club and their lives had been turned upside down with the subsequent events. Even thinking about the murder all these months later made Rose shiver. How could she ever forget finding her friend's body slumped over the grave with a crossbow bolt pierced through her body?

Thankfully they had had a quietish winter to recover, although there had also been the upheaval of Jessica, their oldest daughter, who had dropped the bombshell that her marriage to Rob was on the rocks. Fortunately, that had proved to be a storm in a teacup and after only a three-day separation, Rob had rushed in and declared his undying love to Jessica and had whisked their daughter and grandchildren away.

. . .

NOW ROSE and Tom were preparing to look after Abby and Ella over the March Break while Rob and Jessica had a second honeymoon in Cuba. *Let's just hope that Anne has had her baby before then and not while Abby and Ella are staying with us,* Rose thought as she looked more closely at Cynthia McArdle.

At first glance she appeared to be a young thing in her twenties, but then, on closer inspection Rose realized that she was looking at a very good face lift. The tell-tale tucks at the side of her face were the giveaway, plus her neck, which she garnished with a colourful scarf. Rose glanced at Cynthia's hands, another age giveaway. She now reassessed her age at somewhere over fifty. She realized with a jolt that Cynthia had been speaking to her. She shook her head and smiled saying,

"I'm so sorry. I was miles away in Halifax thinking about our daughter. Forgive me for not listening. Oh, by the way, did Peggy offer you accommodation with us tonight? I've made up the guest room. If you don't mind being around dogs, we would love to have you spend the night."

Cynthia beamed a fantastic smile showing small, pearly white teeth. She was a strange looking woman, not conventionally attractive but certainly quite enigmatic in her own way.

"I would love to take you up on your kind offer. It would only be for tonight as I was planning, weather permitting of course, to go and visit my aunt in Clinton. I promised her that I wouldn't leave this area without a visit. My plane back to Halifax doesn't actually leave until Tuesday."

They were interrupted by the band arriving. By now it was almost seven-thirty. *They are cutting it a bit fine*, Rose thought as she watched the four-man band walk in carrying their guitars and gear, stamping snow off their shoes, and laughing amongst themselves. From snippets of conversation, they had obviously had a few beers at The Albion before coming to the Town Hall.

THE FOUR MEN, two of them in their fifties or even early sixties, wore casual blue jeans and black sweatshirts. Three of the men had shoulder length hair and looked distinctly like aging hippies. The youngest of the band reminded Rose of their son, Paul. He looked about the same age and had a pleasant freshness about him. Rose instantly recognised Joe Berry, the lead singer.

He looked more like George Clooney now with his salt and pepper hair and rugged face. He was still a heart stopper. If their daughter Anne was around, she would say that Joe was 'fit', but maybe not, as he was probably too old for her generation.

Peggy welcomed them effusively and asked Rose if she could show the band downstairs where they had set out sandwiches and beer for them.

"Follow me", Rose said, and the four men traipsed downstairs with Rose in the lead.

"The washrooms are here," she said pointing to the side of the hallway. "Men's are to the left and women's to the right. Of course, you don't really need to know that. You can use any of them," she added to a chuckle from Joe.

They continued to walk through the hallway towards the back where the meeting room was located.

"The kitchen is here. There are glasses on the shelves if you want some water although we have laid out refreshments on the table for you."

When they entered the meeting room, Cynthia McArdle jumped up and made a bee line to greet Joe Berry.

"It's been a long time, Joe," she said. Rose interrupted them before she could say anything else.

"Right, well, if you need anything, I'll be upstairs. See you all later." With that she went to leave. It was already very late. She should have been taking tickets at the door by now.

Rose saw Tom putting glasses out on a tray in the kitchen as she was returning upstairs. She waved to him and almost bumped into Gillian Jeffries making her way downstairs.

"WE MEET AGAIN, Gillian. Can I help you? Are you looking for anything?"

Gillian's face was flushed, and her eyes looked wild. She nodded quickly and said that she was looking for the washroom. Rose pointed the way and continued on her way upstairs to take up her position collecting tickets.

The hall soon started to fill up. There were a number of people that Rose knew mostly from the Croquet Club. She spotted Lena, from the Historical Society, and Angela, the librarian. She looked around to see if she could find Gillian Jeffries but there appeared to be no sign of her yet. Cynthia was about to go on the stage to start her performance. Rose wondered why Gillian was taking so long to return. Was she with Tom?

Tom had just finished loading up his second tray of glasses when he was halted in his tracks by the sound of voices. There were two people arguing out in the hallway besides the kitchen. He recognized right away the voice of Gilly, but the other, a man's voice, he could not place.

He couldn't hear what they were saying, but it certainly did not sound like a friendly discussion. Then it went very quiet, and Tom felt that he could leave the kitchen undetected and carry the glasses upstairs.

As he walked into the hall, he bumped into one of the band members coming out of the men's washroom. Tom smiled at him and continued on his way upstairs. He glanced at his watch as he put the tray of glasses onto the bar table. It was eight-ten and Cynthia the harpist was in full swing. The gentle, rippling music gripped the audience and Tom could see that Cynthia was certainly very professional.

Rose sidled up to Tom and asked if he had seen Gillian Jeffries. He whispered that yes, she had been downstairs arguing with someone, but he didn't know where she had got to after that incident. Rose looked at her watch. It was almost 8:30 p.m. The Berries would soon be on stage.

Cynthia played on and the audience quietened as they were captured by the gentle rhythmic plucking of the harp's strings. She played beautifully and with such feeling. Rose was lulled by the last melody. It seemed to be a combination of *Greensleeves* intermingled with a Celtic beat, an unusual mix but very haunting. Rose was prodded out of her reveries by Peggy who looked agitated. Immediately Rose could see that something was wrong.

"Rose, please come out into the lobby. I need to talk to you," she whispered.

Rose quickly exited the auditorium and met Peggy in the lobby by the front door.

"What's up, Peggy?"

She looked a nervous wreck.

"Joe Berry has gone missing and they're meant to be performing in a few minutes."

Rose thought quickly.

"Well, when Cynthia's finished, we can have a short intermission and hopefully Joe will turn up by then. Has anyone seen him?"

Peggy answered quickly. "Yes, I spoke to him when he

first arrived and then you took the whole band downstairs and that was the last time that I saw him."

"He seemed in good spirits and the rest of the group all appeared quite relaxed." Rose said while she tried to remember what was actually said when she had showed them around.

"Peggy, I presume that you've looked outside? He might have gone out for a cigarette?"

Peggy answered that they had indeed looked outside, and no, he wasn't anywhere to be found. Bill Branson, the lead guitarist, was the only band member that smoked, and he had stepped outside for a cigarette at around eight o'clock.

Cynthia concluded her last piece of music and the curtains closed to tremendous applause. Peggy dashed back into the auditorium and announced that there would be a fifteen-minute intermission. Hopefully, that would be time enough to locate Joe Berry.

Peggy and Rose both went downstairs while Tom continued to pour out the wine and take orders from the audience. Both Rose and Tom had taken the online Smart Serve course and were, therefore, allowed to work on the cash bar. The Town Hall committee had applied for the liquor license one month before. Susan and Jeff, both long time committee members who held their Smart Serve accreditation, had gone away as snowbirds for the winter leaving no one on the committee legitimately allowed to man the bar. That was when Rose had volunteered Tom and herself to take the online course and now they were in great demand.

IT WAS Peggy who found him. He had been pushed into the tiny jail in the Town Hall basement. A kitchen knife protruded from his neck. Blood had splattered everywhere. It was the iron-tinged smell of the copious amounts of blood that had first drawn Peggy to peer into the old jail in the basement.

Rose was closest to her when she let out a piercing scream, a noise so curdled that Rose fairly shook with fear herself. She had run over from the washrooms and found Peggy ashen faced and quivering in shock as she pointed her shaking finger towards the jail room. Rose had run over but had been halted in her steps by the sight before her. It was Joe's eyes that she would see repeatedly in her dreams over the next few weeks.

They seemed to be fixed on her in an accusing way. His mouth was clamped shut and his one hand gripped the knife handle as if he was trying to pull the deadly weapon out. He was clearly dead. Rose recognized the knife as one that the Town Hall had bought in a bid to revamp the kitchen. Indeed, it looked very much like one of the set that Rose herself had purchased only two weeks ago from Kulpeppers in Goderich.

"Oh my gosh, Peggy, oh my gosh. umm... I'll call the police." Rose stammered. She might as well have been talking to herself, as Peggy just stood there in a trance like state. Rose pulled out her phone and tapped in the numbers, 911. A computer voice answered, "Which service are you calling?"

ROSE HALF WHISPERED, "A man is dead. We'll need an ambulance and the police. Please come quickly."

After providing the location and her name she put her phone away and went over to Peggy. She wrapped her arms around her and gently guided her into the meeting room where the three remaining band members were sitting. In a dead pan voice Peggy quietly said, "I'm afraid we have some bad news. I found Joe, but it appears that he has been murdered. I have to go upstairs to make an announcement to the audience, but the police have been called and I am sure that they will want you all to stay here."

Peggy shook her head as if shaking away the horror of the scene she had just witnessed. She turned to leave and then suddenly slumped as if all her energy had evaporated. She spoke softly to Rose with a quivering voice. "Would you mind Rose, telling everyone what's happened. I really don't feel up to it. I feel quite faint. Thank you my dear."

Rose fetched a glass of water from the kitchen and turned to leave The Berries and Peggy sitting in shocked silence. She raced upstairs, being careful not to look at the jail, and found Tom working feverishly taking people's orders.

Doug had volunteered to help, and the two men poured out wine and handed out beers like professional bar men. Rose walked up to the stage picked up the microphone which had been set up for Cynthia the harpist.

"Ummm... good evening everyone. I have an unpleasant announcement to make. The Berries will not be able to perform tonight due to tragic circumstances."

Rose felt her voice thicken and tears spring to her eyes, but she soldiered on. "The lead singer has been found dead and the police are on their way. Please, nobody can leave the hall as I'm sure that that the police will want to question everybody."

Rose took a moment to look around the auditorium. She could see Gillian Jeffries looking in an obvious state of shock. She must have come into the auditorium while Rose was helping Peggy look for Joe Berry because she was certain she was not there before. There was a general murmur of shocked whispers as people settled back in their chairs waiting for the police to arrive. Tom beckoned to Rose who walked over to him in a daze. He put his arms around her and pulled her close to him.

"Are you alright, my love? You look dreadful. Was it you who found Joe?"

"No, Peggy found him and she's in an awful state. Oh Tom, it was horrendous. I cannot get rid of the image of him all covered in blood with a knife protruding from his neck. His dead eyes just stared accusingly at me." Rose felt her voice quiver as big, glistening tears started to roll down her cheeks. *I must try to hold it together*, she thought as she fished in her pocket for a tissue. Taking a big gulp of air, Rose wiped her eyes and asked Tom for a glass of wine.

WHEN SUSAN RECEIVED the call from the Goderich O.P.P. detachment she couldn't believe it. Another murder in Bayfield! It had been less than six months since she had investigated the murders of Mary Stokes and Michael Powell. How could such a small village harbour so much evil? With that thought in mind Susan had grabbed her bag and jumped into her car prepared to drive the eighty-minute journey from her house in Wortley Village, London, up to Bayfield.

The air was crisp and fresh snow had fallen covering the roads like fine talcum powder. *At least it wasn't a blizzard*, thought Susan who was used to driving in all weather conditions. Hopefully she would arrive at the Town Hall before ten o'clock.

Just over an hour later as she pulled into Clan Gregor Square, Susan was amazed at the activity in front of the Town Hall. An ambulance stood immediately in front with its lights flashing, which Susan found ironic as this was after all, a dead body, not an emergency.

Yellow police tape, fluttering in the wind, marked off

the whole front of the Town Hall and police officers kitted out in disposable white coveralls with hoods and masks, were already going about their business. Susan searched for somewhere to park. She finally plumbed for parking in front of Brandon's Hardware Store and walked over to the Town Hall. She was about to pass under the yellow tape when an officer came over and blocked her entry. Susan recoiled. She had never been stopped from entering a crime scene before.

She fished in her bag for her warrant card and held it up to the Constable. "I'm Inspector Parker from Serious Crimes and I have driven all the way from London to be here tonight. I could have left it until tomorrow, but in murder cases it is imperative to see the scene of the crime first-hand before it gets tampered. I sincerely hope that your team of men have not tampered with the evidence. Now please, let me through. I have work to do."

The officer stood back and ushered her through.

As Susan entered the building, the crime scene photographer was just leaving. They almost bumped into each other. Susan grabbed his arm.

"Excuse me; I don't think that we've met before. My name is Detective Inspector Susan Parker, I will be leading this investigation and so I would appreciate it if you could make sure I get copies of the photographs forwarded to me. I expect we will be setting up an Incident Room in the village"

The man looked somewhat taken aback, but he politely held out his hand and said, "My name is Peter Joyce. I was asked by the Goderich O.P.P. Detachment to come out to record the scene of the crime. I always like to use a traditional SLR with roll film as well as a digital camera. I'm of the old school; digital can get deleted or played around with whereas traditional film photography never tells lies."

He smiled and suddenly his face changed from just ordinary to amazingly handsome. Susan's heart missed a beat.

"Oh, well, if you can get the photographs to me as soon as possible that would be great. Here's my card with my contact particulars and a secure email address. Now I must go and see with my own eyes what horrors await."

PETER JOYCE LOADED his old Olympus SLR and his modern digital video recorder into his battered, old Jeep. He watched as Susan nodded to the attending officer who took her name and let her through into the hall. DI Susan Parker had intrigued him. He would ask around and find out more about the attractive woman who commanded such a senior position in the police force.

As she entered the hall, Susan had glanced over towards the fire hall and the neighbouring Lion's building which, in the past, she had been able to use as an incident room.

It was a convenient location, and she crossed her fingers that if needed it would once again be available for her use.

The poster in the glass display box by the front door of the Town Hall showed four men, older men at that, with the name The Berries. A 'Sold-Out' sticker had been stapled over the poster. She walked into the Town Hall and was immediately hit by a stream of heat. Susan undid her thick overcoat and walked up the steps to where her old friend Rose Blair stood talking to her husband, Tom. There was something about Tom that Susan found immensely attractive and she wasn't quite sure what it was.

He wasn't conventionally handsome, and he wasn't overtly manly, but the chemistry between them ignited whenever she was near him and somehow, she could not quell it. Rose turned from Tom and seeing Susan, rushed over to greet her, making Susan instantly feel guilty about her thoughts for Tom.

She had been best friends with Rose all through their university days spent at Queens in Kingston. After graduation they had both gone their separate ways, Rose to Tom and a happy marriage, Susan to a disastrous relationship followed by a divorce and a major change of career.

She had crawled up the ladder, a predominantly male one at that, and had reached the position of Detective Inspector by sheer hard work and tenacity alone and was now getting close to retirement. Susan smiled warmly at her friend Rose.

"Susan, I wish that we didn't always have to meet under such dreadful circumstances. How are you?"

Out of the corner of her eye, Rose noticed a flash of light sparkle from Susan's finger. "Oh my gosh, Susan! You're wearing an engagement ring!"

Susan blushed as she waved her hand in front of her friend. "Henri and I got engaged at Christmas. But right now, dear Rose, I must get to work. I'll tell you all about it later. Now, show me the body."

The two women went downstairs to the jail. The investigation into Joe Berry's death had begun.

TWO

I t had been a long night for Tom and Rose. They did not get home until well past midnight and, as a result, had slept in the following morning. When they got up, a winter's wonderland greeted them. At least four inches of snow blanketed the outside world. Ben and Puff, their trusted dogs, had slept in, and were let out into the snow laden yard and instantly started to dig and bury themselves. Rose laughed as Puff disappeared in a cloud of snow and Ben chased his tail around and around in circles. *Just like little children,* thought Rose as she fried up some bacon and mushrooms for their breakfast.

For a brief moment, the events of the previous night had been forgotten until the stillness of the moment was broken by the shrill ring of their house telephone. Tom was still getting up, so Rose walked over into the lounge to answer it. It was Anne, their daughter from Halifax.

"MOM, oh Mom, my contractions have started. Alan's just gone to get the car started. I'm having a baby."

Rose clapped her hands with excitement and called out to Tom. "Tom! Tom, Anne's in labour." She then went back to talking to their daughter.

"Now, Anne, you could be in for a long wait. They will tell you how far dilated you are when the doctor does his examination. Just stay calm and be prepared for a strenuous time ahead."

Rose didn't like to tell her daughter how awful labour could be. There was no point. She would soon find out for herself and really nobody could prepare anyone for what lies ahead.

"Get Alan to phone us when things really get going. Just hold in there darling."

Rose put the phone down and continued cooking their breakfast. *Another grandchild, how precious,* she thought, *what perfect timing.* The baby would be born, and she would be home in time for March break.

Tom appeared all freshly showered and shaved. He came up to Rose and kissed her gently on her cheek.

"I'm not going to the fitness centre today, love, it's Saturday. I'll go on the computer and see if I can get you on a flight to Halifax for tomorrow."

"Perfect darling. Now I must give Peggy a call and see what is happening at the Town Hall."

TOM LET the dogs back inside and poured out some kibbles which they both wolfed down with gusto. Puff had settled in so well after his rocky start the previous summer. They had adopted the funny looking shaggy dog, who had been orphaned after his owner, Mary Stokes, Rose's good friend, had been found murdered at the Croquet Club.

Tom overheard Rose exclaim to Peggy on the phone, "Oh, I feel so bad. Cynthia was supposed to have come home with us last night, but with all the chaos, I completely forgot about her. Thank you, Peggy for taking her back with you. Yes. We can have her stay with us tonight. No problem."

Rose put the receiver down and sighed deeply.

"Oh Tom, I forgot all about Cynthia. Peggy took her home last night, but she has guests coming to stay today, so I said that Cynthia could come and stay with us for a few days."

Tom nodded, but then he remembered the flight that he had just booked for Rose. He had managed to get her onto a flight out of London to Halifax the next day.

"Rose, she can only stay tonight as you leave tomorrow, and she probably won't want to stay without you being here. Didn't she say something about an aunt in Clinton?"

"Yes, you're right. She can go to Clinton tomorrow. Now it's time that I tidied up the kitchen and prepared something for our dinner tonight. What have you got on today, my love?"

Tom pondered awhile. He had been tempted to say that he would go for a run, but anything to do with fitness appeared to be a sensitive issue at the moment.

"I THINK that I'll take the dogs for a walk and maybe pop into the library."

Rose barely heard him as she had disappeared into the pantry looking for ingredients to make her seafarers pie.

Tom smiled to himself. *That's my girl*, he thought,

cooking away the blues. It was the best tonic for Rose. When stressed out, she always turned to baking.

GARY, the President of the Lion's Club had been more than helpful when Susan had placed her call that morning. Yes, she could use the Lion's Hall for the duration of the investigation. He would meet her there at 9:00 a.m. to hand over the keys. She had also been successful in booking the same room as the previous summer at The Bayfield Village Inn and had already gone for an early morning swim in the lovely indoor pool which left her feeling thoroughly invigorated and ready to face the first day of the murder inquiry.

Susan drove to The Lion's Hall and parked her car. She noticed two O.P.P. cruisers parked by her side. Hopefully P.C. Brown and P.C. Elliot would have been seconded to her. They had both proved themselves invaluable last year and had earned her respect for their diligence and sheer hard work. She had requested that Sergeant Flowers and P.C. Mathieson from London Serious Crimes Division also be seconded to her for the length of the case.

Susan was relieved to see Gary talking to Constables. Brown and Elliot. The hall had been unlocked and someone had already set up a white board.

"Good morning," Gary said as he stretched out his hand to shake Susan's. "I was at the concert last night myself and was so looking forward to seeing The Berries. I'm a great fan of them. What a rum thing to happen!" Gary shook his head and looked gravely at Susan.

Susan glanced at her watch and replied a bit impatiently, "Hopefully we will get to the bottom of this quickly. Thanks for responding so efficiently to my call, Gary." She said willing Gary to leave so that she could start her briefing.

Sergeant Flowers and P.C. Mathieson had not yet arrived. The weather was still brutally cold, but at least there were no snowstorms forecast for a few days. *Come on you two,* Susan thought as she politely smiled at Gary Longsworth.

As if in answer to her prayer a black car pulled up outside the Lion's Hall and her two officers stepped out. This was her cue to say goodbye to Gary and welcome in the team.

Finally, she was ready to start the briefing.

"Good morning, gentlemen. No need for any formal introductions as we all know each other from last year's investigation. Now here are the facts as we know them from last night.

The Berries were booked to perform at the Town Hall to be accompanied by Cynthia McArdle, a harpist from Halifax. According to Peggy Grierson, the chairperson of the Town Hall committee, the band members were in good spirits when they arrived, and everyone was relieved that they had made the drive from Toronto in that horrible snowstorm that we had yesterday.

Apparently, they arrived around 6:00 p.m. and had dinner at The Albion. Afterwards they walked over to the Town Hall and made themselves comfortable in the meeting room downstairs. Peggy said that she couldn't find Joe Berry. When she started to get alarmed around 8:15 p.m., Cynthia McArdle, the harpist, had started performing at 8:00 p.m. and the band was due to go on stage at 8:30 p.m.

Joe Berry was found at 8:40 stuffed in the small jail situated just opposite of the kitchen. He had a knife protruding through his neck, a particularly nasty stabbing. Forensics were there for two hours last night and the police photographer, Peter Joyce, videoed the crime scene as well as took photographs.

They have promised to send their reports and photographs through as quickly as they can.

Now men, we have an awful lot of interviewing to do. There were at least a hundred people at the Town Hall last night, many of them out-of-towners. They were all asked to leave their names and contact numbers before they left, but I'll be surprised if we managed to get everyone. I know that there were a number of empty seats in the auditorium when I arrived, and Peggy told me that it had been a sold-out performance.

Sergeant Flowers, I would like you to interview the three remaining band members, Cynthia McArdle, and their close relatives. Leave no stone unturned. They are not to leave the village until I'm satisfied that we have all the information and background checks recorded thoroughly. Constable Mathieson, can you interview Tom and Rose Blair who were at the scene of the crime, oh and also a Miss Gillian Jeffries who was overheard arguing with Joe Berry sometime around 8:00
p.m. I would like Constables Brown and Elliot to systematically contact and interview everyone else who was at the concert. Right. Any questions?"

THERE WAS total silence in the room as the men digested the information. Sergeant Flowers coughed and stood up looking thoughtful as he said, "Is anyone going to interview the Town Hall Committee members? This Peggy person was certainly around at the time of the murder and there probably were a number of other committee members at the concert too."

Susan answered quickly. "Well, that will be my job to interview the committee members. Okay men, get to it. Same time tomorrow morning and I want to hear some positive results."

The officers cleared the room quietly leaving Susan to turn on her laptop and fire off a report to H.Q. in London. She then sent out a press release to The London Free Press, The Goderich Star, and The Clinton Herald. With that all done she sent a text message to Henri, who was a Detective Inspector in the Section des Crimes Contre la Surete du Quebec. He was also her fiancé although a wedding date had yet to be settled. They had met almost two years previous when she had been working on the murder on Bayfield beach case, which had involved the Montreal Mobsters, thus the connection to Henri le Bruin.

Their paths had crossed a number of times in work related cases, but it was only after Susan had almost been killed last summer when working the murder at the Croquet Club case, that their relationship had taken on a deeper meaning. On Christmas Eve, Henri had proposed to Susan and she had accepted.

That was two months ago, and she had only seen him three times since their engagement. One of them would have to move to be closer. Susan was reluctant to give up her newly bought house in Wortley Village to move to Montreal. She was ready to retire but not ready to move away from her lovely home.

Henri lived in a condo in Verdun, a rather soulless unit which Susan could not bear to live in. If it came to it, she would be prepared to move to be with Henri, but they would have to find a new home together somewhere other than Verdun. Neither of them had confronted the issue and so an impasse had been reached.

· · ·

SUSAN TEXTED Henri and suggested that he might like to come down for what was left of the weekend and join her at The Bayfield Village Inn. The thought of him always made Susan feel all warm inside. The chemistry between them was amazing.

Susan wondered though whether their relationship was only about the absolute delicious sex that they shared together or whether they really had anything else in common. That was the trouble with only snatched weekends together, most of which was spent in bed, what did they really know about each other?

Susan brushed the negative thoughts away as she closed her phone and collected up her notes. She would start with interviewing Peggy Grierson, the Chairperson of the Town Hall Committee.

CYNTHIA MCARDLE WAS DROPPED off at Rose and Tom's house by Peggy Grierson shortly before lunch that Saturday. She wore a thick red cloak and a bright purple woollen beret, black fleece lined knee length boots adorned her legs which poked out like sticks beneath a thick, long woollen skirt. *She looked like a lass from one of Thomas Hardy's novels*, thought Rose as she opened the door and waved to Peggy before welcoming Cynthia into their home.

"This is lovely!" Cynthia exclaimed as she took off her boots and handed her thick cloak to Rose.

"Well, it is rather quiet at the moment as Tom is out with the dogs. Just be warned that Puff and Ben think that everyone comes to visit them and will greet you rather effusively. Come into the kitchen and I'll make us some lunch."

Cynthia followed Rose into their snug and cosy kitchen. Rose had just finished making a batch of oatmeal cookies and had been in the middle of putting together a quiche when the doorbell rang.

"Would you like a cup of tea, Cynthia?" Rose asked as she filled the kettle, put it on the stove and finished grating cheese for the top of the quiche. "I've just finished making this quiche and it won't take long to cook. Tom should be back soon so we can all sit down for lunch then. Now, what do you take in your tea?"

Cynthia hadn't been able to get a word in edgeways.

Although she found Rose very friendly, the woman could certainly talk. She herself, was if anything, quite shy even verging on introvert. Words did not come easily, whereas music flowed effortlessly through her fingers when she played the harp.

She looked around the open plan kitchen which opened on to a cosy sitting room. There was a framed photograph of a family group on the far wall and Cynthia could recognize her hosts, Rose and Tom.

"Those must be your children," Cynthia said pointing to the picture.

Rose looked up and nodded saying, 'Yes. Jessica is our oldest, then Paul, and Anne who now lives in Halifax. In fact, I'm flying out there tomorrow. She's having a baby and I'd promised to go out and help for a week after the baby's birth."

"WHEREABOUTS IN HALIFAX DOES SHE LIVE?" Cynthia asked.

Rose thought for a minute. She had yet to visit Anne since she had moved in with Alan. They actually lived across from Halifax in Dartmouth on Pine Street. Both of them worked at Dalhousie University and took the ferry from Dartmouth to Halifax every day to work.

That much Rose knew but realised that she actually knew very little about Halifax or Dartmouth.

"Oh, that's so funny," Cynthia said after Rose had told her Anne's address. "I live just around the corner on Myrtle Street, not far from Dartmouth Common."

"Do you live alone, Cynthia?" Rose asked, trying not to appear too prying.

Cynthia paused and seemed to withdraw into herself before answering.

"Yes, I live alone now. My father died ten years ago, and I've spent that time looking after my mother who died this past year. I inherited the house on Myrtle Street."

Before Rose could reply, Tom, followed by Puff and Ben, entered the kitchen. The dogs charged over to Cynthia, wagging their tails eager to meet their new guest. Tom marched over and extended his hand to Cynthia.

"Pleased to meet you again. Has Rose shown you your room yet?"

Rose let out a little yelp. "Oh my gosh, I do apologise, Cynthia. I haven't shown you your room or anything. Please forgive me. Now follow me and then we'll come back for lunch. The quiche is almost ready."

Tom looked at Rose. She was behaving slightly odd and as for Cynthia, what a strange looking woman. Her long woollen skirt and shapeless tunic top, not to mention the thick braid of hair which made her look like a woman from another century.

TOM SET the table while the women were in the bedroom. He also got out the makings of a salad and was in the middle of slicing up some cucumber when the women returned.

'Tom, my love, it's been five hours since Anne called. Do you think she's okay?"

"Of course she is, darling. She's having a baby. Remember how long you were in labour with all of our three? No, Alan will call just as soon as the baby is born. Don't worry. Now, what else should I put in this salad?"

Cynthia patted Ben on his head, rather tentatively. Rose thought that she obviously was not used to dogs. They all sat down to a pleasant lunch. Soon the conversation steered towards the murder. It was Tom who opened the Pandora's Box.

"Did you know Joe Berry very well, Cynthia?"

She turned physically ashen at the mention of his name and stopped eating abruptly.

"Are you feeling alright?" Rose asked, a worried frown appearing on her forehead. Cynthia paused before answering quietly.

"Yes, I'm quite okay. It's just that I don't want to think about last night."

Tom, unperturbed, continued on, oblivious to Rose's look of warning.

"Have you often played the supporting role for The Berries? I got the impression that you knew them quite well."

Cynthia's mouth formed a tight line and her eyes seemed to have turned to stone. She stood up and very politely, but firmly, asked to be excused and then rushed off to her bedroom.

"Honestly Tom, you are sometimes so tactless. Couldn't you see that she was visibly upset?"

Tom just shrugged his shoulders and continued eating his lunch quietly thinking to himself that Cynthia had overreacted to a normal question. A few minutes later Rose smiled and kissed Tom on his cheek and said,

"I reckon that she must have known the band really well to react that way. She's slightly weird, and I cannot quite put my finger on what it is about her that makes me feel so unsettled."

Tom patted Rose's hand and got up from the table. "Well, it's a good thing that you're going away love, otherwise you'd be poking your nose into police business again. Remember last year? No, you need to keep out of this, darling, and concentrate now on our new grandchild."

But I don't leave until tomorrow, Rose thought as she cleared away the dishes. There would be no harm in asking a few questions and she knew exactly whom she wanted to talk to.

SUSAN WALKED down Main Street and was amazed at how quiet it was considering it was Saturday. It was like a ghost town. The street looked positively beautiful all covered in snow. Surreal was the word that popped into her mind.

If the shops were all closed Susan knew of one place that would be open and that was the library. She had gotten to know the librarian, Angela, quite well from past investigations in the village. Angela knew everyone and seemed to have her finger on the pulse of the village. Susan stopped outside DaVinci's, her favourite coffee shop, although it was no longer a coffee shop but a restaurant now. It was actually open for lunch that day and Susan was sorely tempted to pop in, but work called first. Maybe afterwards she might have a bite to eat.

The library was open and fairly buzzing with people. *So, this is where everyone meets,* Susan thought as she entered the warm building. It had started to snow quite heavily outside and between 10 to 15 centimetres had been forecast for that day. She shook off her coat and stamped the snow off her boots before going up to the counter. Angela was busy checking out a whole stack of books belonging to a frail old lady who looked to be in her hundreds. *Would she even be able to carry the huge pile of books*, Susan thought as she edged her way up to the counter.

ANGELA LOOKED up and seeing Susan gave her a dazzling, welcoming smile.

"Hi, it's Susan, isn't it? I remember you from last summer. Now let me guess, you're here because of the murder at the Town Hall?" There seemed to be a twinkle in her eyes as she spoke.

"Yes, well, much as I love Bayfield, I seem only to be here under such circumstances. Actually, I wanted to have a quick word with you when you have a minute."

Angela smiled again and turned back to serve another lady at the check-out counter. "I'll be right with you, just give me a minute."

Susan looked around the beautiful library. There were comfortable armchairs and a sofa arranged around a stone fireplace which looked really inviting. Two of the chairs were taken with people reading newspapers. Susan sat down on the sofa and opened up her laptop. She had typed in the names of a few of the Town Hall committee members but still needed the completed list. She was hoping that Angela would be able to supply her with that information. Peggy Grierson was the Chairperson, and she knew that her friend Rose was also a member, but those were the only names she had on her list so far. She had already spoken to Peggy, but that was last night when the woman was clearly still in a state of shock and couldn't talk coherently. She was first on her list to interview.

Angela tapped Susan on her shoulder and told her that she was available to talk for five minutes while there was a lull in the traffic of patrons and books.

"Thanks, Angela," Susan said. "Basically I wanted to ask you if you had a list of the Town Hall committee members?"

Angela thought for a minute and then went back to the counter. She returned with a Town Hall brochure. Listed on the back were the names of the committee members.

"This is last year's brochure so there might be a few changes on the Board, but it will give you an idea. Oh, but you know that an awful lot of them are snowbirds, so you'll probably find that they are not around to be questioned."

Susan took the brochure and was about to leave when she turned around and said,

"Were you a fan of The Berries?"

Angela laughed, "Oh, no, I'm more of a heavy metal gal, but I know that they had a huge following here in Bayfield." Angela lowered her voice to a whisper as she continued, "It is rumoured that Gillian Jeffries, our local fitness instructor, had a relationship with Joe Berry some years ago. She owns Time for Toning, up by The Black Dog. You could start there as I'm sure that Gillian will have loads to say about Joe Berry."

Interesting, Susan thought, *how the local villagers knew so much.* Experience had taught her that if you listened to the local gossip generally much information could be gathered for any investigation. She thanked Angela and left the library.

The band had been booked into the Little Inn. She had assigned Sergeant Flowers the job of interviewing the band members. Constable Mathieson had been tasked with interviewing the fitness guru, Gillian Jeffries. It would be interesting to see if she owned up to having had a relationship with the deceased. That still left the Town Hall committee members to contact, starting first with Peggy Grierson.

Susan pulled out her iPhone and was just about to give Peggy a call when her phone rang. It was Henri returning her text message. He would be in Bayfield tomorrow evening and asked if she could reserve a table at The Black Dog.

Susan's heart gave a little flutter at the thought of being with Henri again. He always had that effect on her, irrational and so out of character. Susan always felt like a lovesick adolescent when it came to Henri.

Walking up Main Street Susan could count on her fingers the number of shops that were open: The Bayfield General Store, DaVinci's, the Optometrist, Martin Arts, Headhunter's Hairdressers, the real estate offices, the Black Dog, and the Albion. Everything else was closed and locked up for the duration of the winter.

SUSAN GOT through to Peggy Grierson and arranged to meet her at 2:30 p.m. giving her enough time to grab a bite to eat for lunch. DaVinci's was still open. Susan walked in and ordered a chicken and bacon wrap and a large coffee. She eyed the carrot cake greedily but abstained from ordering.

She had to watch her weight as Henri seemed to like her the way she was. Fortunately for Susan, she had been born with lean genes. Both her parents had tended towards thinness even in their old age and both had good appetites and longevity.

·   ·   ·

PEGGY GRIERSON LIVED the other side of the river at Harbour Court. She had bought her condo five years previous after retiring from Brampton, where her husband Reg had worked as an Actuary for London Life. Peggy had been a teacher. It had been their dream to buy a boat and a condo and move to Bayfield. They loved everything about the village and were totally involved with the community.

Susan pulled up to the visitor's parking lot and jumped out of her car. She looked around at the condo's trying to find number 109. It was a very attractive development, she thought as she surveyed the units around her. *Maybe Henri and I could buy one and retire to Bayfield,* Susan thought. Bittersweet memories of Jim Reynolds and her brief fling living together down by the river at the Bayfield Cottage Colony, came flooding back to her. Maybe, settling in Bayfield would not be the best of ideas for Henri and her, not yet anyway.

Ringing the doorbell, Susan once again took in her surroundings. No two units were completely alike. Peggy Grierson's home was an end of terrace unit and appeared more spacious than others. Peggy answered the door looking immeasurably better than she had the night before.

"Hi, Peggy. Do you mind if I come in? I've just got a few questions to ask. It shouldn't take long."

PEGGY NODDED and gestured with her hand for Susan to follow. In the sitting room a man lay fast asleep on the couch. Peggy put her finger to her lips and then beckoned Susan to follow her downstairs to a delightful family room.

"Sorry about that. Reg hasn't been at all well lately. He just wants to sleep. Now, how can I help you?"

Susan got out her notebook.

"Could you tell me when The Berries were actually booked to perform at the Town Hall?"

Peggy thought for a minute. "We booked them a couple of months before Christmas, just after Thanksgiving if I remember correctly."

"Had you ever met Joe Berry before the concert?"

"No, other than emailing him I had never any physical contact. To be honest they were not a band that I particularly liked, but the rest of the committee were really quite excited about the booking. They felt quite honoured that The Berries had agreed to come to Bayfield of all places!"

"I must admit that I had wondered how you had enticed them here. Did any of the band members have any connection to the village?"

Peggy looked undecided and paused before answering Susan's question.

"Well...I'm not one to repeat gossip but Val, our treasurer, told me that Gillian Jeffries, the owner of Time for Toning, had been seeing Joe Berry on and off for a number of years. That could be your connection to the village."

Susan wrote it all down and once again thought how much Gillian could reveal when being interviewed by Constable Mathieson.

"So, as I understand, Val is your treasurer. And I see from this committee list that Julie is your secretary. Were both women at the concert last night?"

PEGGY SHOOK her head before answering. "You know Susan, only two of the committee members were there last night which I found disappointing considering all the hype when we initially booked the band. It is February and over half of our board have gone south to Florida or Mexico. We barely have a quorum at our meetings these days. Rose and I were the only committee members there last night as well as Tom, Rose's husband, who kindly manned the bar."

"Could you give me the names of the committee members who have not joined the snowbirds and who were in the village last night?"

Peggy thought for a minute and then held up her fingers as she counted off the names.

"Bill, he couldn't come last night as his daughter was visiting from B.C. Karen, she's been laid up with flu this whole week. Then there's Jack. I'm not sure why he didn't come, but I know that he wasn't a Berry fan. Lastly, there is Betty and she's just had foot surgery and has to use crutches for a while. The rest of the committee won't be back before April.

We are a very busy group and during the winter months we run on empty for much of the time. Take next weekend. We have our annual Soups On event which over the years has become very popular. It is Family Day weekend and so there are loads of visitors to the village. Bill, Jack, Rose, and I will be the only one of us to be around to organise and orchestrate everything. It's an awful lot of work you know."

Susan had never sat on any volunteer committees before. She was paid to represent the police on a number of different boards but volunteering freely was somewhat alien to her.

"You must love what you do otherwise why would you do it?"

Peggy paused again, her intelligent face crunching up into a frown.

"Yes, well, we all love the village but sometimes it feels as if it's the same people doing everything. I'm just a bit worn down at the moment so don't listen to me."

Susan bit the end of her pen and turned her notebook over.

"Well, I'm sorry to be wearing you down even further, but I do need you to recall the events of last night. You were too traumatized to say too much before, but I do need to take your statement. Let's start from when you arrived at the Town Hall shall we?"

Peggy quietly went through the order of events leading up to the macabre finding of the body. She stopped abruptly then and looked up to the ceiling while saying. "I do feel somewhat embarrassed by the way I reacted. I was hysterical and if it wasn't for Rose Blair it would have been sheer pandemonium. I am ashamed of my lack of self-control."

Susan took Peggy's hand and patted it gently. "Don't beat yourself up. You know that ninety percent of people would have reacted just the way you did. Joe Berry was murdered in a particularly gruesome way. Could you tell me about the knife?"

Peggy shook her head and seemed to compose herself. "Yes, it was actually one of a set of new knifes recently purchased from a kitchen shop in Goderich called Kulpeppers. Rose bought the knives just last week. I remember her saying that they were really sharp and to be careful with them."

Susan paused for a minute while she collected her thoughts together.

"All the committee members would have known about the knives?"

"Yes, well those members who were at our last meeting. Jack, Bill, Karen, Betty, Rose, and me. Just the six of us."

"Would the knife have been out of the drawer for any reason, do you know?"

"No. There was no food served at the concert, only beer

and wine. I can't see a reason for any utensils to have been left out. The knives are all kept in the top drawer. Rose bought a set of four and paid $80 for them. I know this because she handed the receipt to me last night so that I could write out a cheque. With our treasurer gone for the winter, I am in charge of writing out cheques. She could possibly have left the package of knives on the counter, but I don't remember seeing them myself."

Susan stood up to leave. "Well, thank you, Peggy. I won't take up any more of your time. If you think of anything else here is my card. Please do not hesitate to call me anytime."

Peggy showed Susan to the door and looked out over the car park at the huge snowflakes now coming down like giant fluffy feathers from the sky.

"Drive carefully," she said as Susan got into her car to drive away.

It would turn out to be a very snowy day.

THREE

Constable Mathieson had spent an interesting half hour at the gym. Gillian Jeffries had agreed to meet him at nine a.m., and it was now 9:20 and still no sign of her. He looked at his watch again and then went back to viewing the gym members working up a sweat.

They were all men, mostly middle aged, some looking horribly out of shape. There was a life-sized poster of an attractive woman working out. She was wearing a black leotard which showed up her curvaceous body fabulously and sported a bright red head band which kept her gorgeous shoulder length auburn hair off her face.

One of the men heavily sweating on an exercise bike had pointed to the poster saying, "That's our Gilly." *So that was Gillian Jeffries,* Constable Mathieson thought, *but where was the real person?*

He had tried phoning her several times and each time he got her voicemail. After a further ten minutes of hanging around, the Constable left the gym. A blast of frigid air hit him as he slipped and slithered on the wooden board walk in front of *Time for Toning*.

He had already decided that in concession to fitness he would walk down to the end of Main Street. Susan had asked Sergeant Flowers to interview the band members.

They had been booked into The Little Inn and he hoped to join up with Sergeant Flowers and maybe grab a coffee if they were still serving breakfast. He left his black police cruiser parked in front of the gym and set off at a fast pace. If the Constable had not been in such a hurry, he might have observed two cold looking dogs tied up to the cast iron fence in front of DaVinci's.

Inside, had he cared to observe, he would have seen Tom Blair holding hands with Gillian Jeffries as she delicately dabbed her beautiful tear-filled eyes with a white hand-kerchief.

TOM AND ROSE had received the call from Alan at ten o'clock the previous evening. Oliver James was born at 9:45 p.m. and mother and baby were doing well.

Tom had opened a bottle of Champagne, and Rose, Cynthia, and he had given a toast to their new grandson.

That was last night and now Rose was anxiously waiting for a phone call from Anne. She wanted to know all the details about the birth.

However, breakfast called. She decided to make a frittata as she wasn't sure what time Cynthia would get up and frit-tatas kept really well in the oven. While she had the oven on, she would also make a batch of orange and cranberry scones.

Humming to herself, Rose chopped up the mushrooms and onions and decided not to add any bacon just in case Cynthia was a vegetarian. She had forgotten to ask. What else could she put into the frittata, thought Rose as she opened the fridge and was just peering inside when Tom walked into the kitchen.

"OH, Tom, you gave me a fright. I'm just looking to see what else I can add to the frittata. It doesn't look very appetizing with just mushrooms and onions."

"Why don't you slice up some potatoes and then it will be more like a Spanish tortilla?"

Rose laughed, "What a great idea. You know, my love, sometimes you are just so inspiring." She kissed him quickly on his cheek.

"I'll put the coffee on and then take the dogs for a walk around the block. Have they been out yet?"

Rose shook her head. Both Ben and Puff were still curled up in their dog beds in Rose and Tom's bedroom. They appeared in no hurry to get up.

Tom looked outside at the winter wonderland. Thick, white, virgin snow lay everywhere. Fluffy cotton wool like clumps hung from the tree branches and snow crystals framed the window. He went to the lobby and put his heavy snow boots on, a thick woollen toque, and jacket, and then picked up the dogs' leashes. He only had to rattle them once and the two dogs came scrambling into the kitchen wide awake and excited at the prospect of a walk.

"I'll be back in about thirty minutes." Tom said as he quickly closed the front door before the icy Arctic air could freeze the house. He set off at a quick pace practically dragging the dogs along beside him. The trouble was that they wanted to stop every few minutes to sniff some wonderful smell and it was definitely far too cold to linger.

Tom walked towards Main Street. If DaVinci's was open

he would grab a coffee to go. He turned onto Charles Street and practically bumped into Gillian Jeffries.

She seemed oblivious to her surroundings and was hardly dressed for the freezing cold. In fact, she looked as if she had slept in her clothes as they appeared all wrinkled. Her beautiful chestnut hair looked unkempt and she wore no makeup. Somehow her fragile vulnerability was more appealing than her normal confident self.

"Gillian, what on earth are you doing out here in the cold without your winter coat and boots? You'll catch a death of a cold. Look, come with me. We'll get a coffee in DaVinci's and you can pour your heart out to me there."

Tom tied up the dogs on the wrought iron fencing. Gillian silently followed him into the coffee shop and there they stayed for the following thirty minutes deep in conversation.

Rose looked at her watch. They were having a very late breakfast. It would be past ten before they would actually eat. *Oh well,* she thought, it is Sunday after all and should be a day of rest. She sliced up three potatoes and continued to fry them in with the onions and mushroom until they were cooked. She then grabbed four eggs and beat them up with some cream and poured the whole lot over the vegetables, transferred it all into a shallow casserole dish and put it in the oven.

Next, she pulled out her food processor and threw in flour, butter, salt, and sugar to make the scones. Slowly she added milk until it was just the texture of pastry. Finally, she added a handful of cranberries and grated the zest of an orange into the mixture. Rose proceeded to roll out and then cut it into scone shapes. Into the oven they went. She then quickly cleared up the mess and then set the table for breakfast. There was still no sign of Cynthia or Tom. It was now nine forty-five.

Tom didn't return with the dogs until after ten and still there was no sign of Cynthia.

"Gosh, you were gone a long time, Tom." Rose said feeling really fed up as she had gone to the trouble of cooking a nice breakfast and first Tom was late and now Cynthia showed no sign of appearing any time soon for breakfast.

Tom didn't say anything but instead busied himself with taking off his boots and coat. He walked over to Rose and gave her a kiss.

"I stopped by DaVinci's and got myself a coffee, love. It's freezing cold outside."

Rose barely listened to his explanation. She seemed very distracted.

"Should I wake her?" Rose said anxiously looking at the Frittata.

Tom rubbed his tummy and said, "Well, I don't know about you, but I'm starving. We'll eat and she can just join us when she wakes up. If she sleeps in, we can always just make her an egg."

They had both finished eating when Cynthia finally appeared. Rose jumped up from the table.

"Would you like some breakfast?"

Cynthia shook her head saying, "Oh, sorry, didn't I tell you, I don't eat breakfast."

Tom didn't want to catch Rose's eye. He could see her visibly bristle as she politely asked Cynthia if she would like some coffee.

"I only drink decaffeinated green tea and I never ever drink coffee."

Rose bristled again, but Tom rescued her quickly by

saying, "I could drive you over to Clinton this morning, say in an hour's time, if that's okay by you?"

Cynthia had just opened her mouth to reply when the telephone rang. Rose answered.

"Oh, hi Susan. Yes. Cynthia is here. Do you want to have a word with her?"

Rose passed the phone over and walked over to Tom. The phone call was brief. Cynthia turned to Rose and Tom and said quite sharply.

"Inspector Parker wants to interview me. Would it be alright if she comes here?"

"Of course she can. Just make yourself at home," Tom said trying not to sound sarcastic.

"She did say that she would like to have a word with you both as well." Cynthia said as she plumped herself down on the sofa.

"Would you like to phone your aunt in Clinton?" Tom asked, "Because I'm more than happy to drive you over after your talk with the Inspector."

"I'll phone her when I'm ready," Cynthia snapped back. Tom had been put in his place in no uncertain terms.

Rose had just cleared away the breakfast table when the doorbell rang. Tom let Susan in and immediately she came over and gave Rose a big hug.

"I can smell those divine scones from down the street. Tell me that you've saved some for me?"

Rose laughed and brought out the Tupperware container that she had just filled with the leftover scones from their breakfast.

"Here you are. I'll butter a couple for you. Do you want some homemade peach jam on them? And I presume you would like a cup of coffee or tea?"

Cynthia listened to their conversation with an open mouth. As soon as she could get a word in, she spoke.

"You two know each other then?"

With a big mouthful of scone Susan answered, "Oh, yes. We go way back. We were at university together."

Swallowing her scone Susan continued, "But enough about me enjoying myself eating Rose's delicious scones. I must ask you some questions. Could you run through your recollections of the evening of the concert starting from when you first arrived in Bayfield?"

Cynthia was about to make some sarcastic remark and then she appeared to check herself in time.

"A friend of mine drove me here from London. I arrived around six and was dropped off at the Town Hall. There was no one around so I lugged my harp up onto the stage and sat and waited for about forty minutes until a woman called Peggy arrived. I asked if I could warm up my harp for ten minutes or so and she said that we had plenty of time, although she was a bit concerned about the band not turning up.

They actually arrived at about seven-twenty by which time I was downstairs nursing a glass of wine. I was introduced to the men.

I HAVE to confess I'm not a particular fan of The Berries. They were popular before my time. I'm more of a classical music girl. I have to say that they were very friendly and the lead singer, Joe Berry was quite charming. Mind you, I barely said a word to them and at seven-fifty I went back upstairs to get ready for my performance. That, I'm afraid, is about all that I can tell you."

Susan had been busy writing Cynthia's statement down, but she looked up at the conclusion and chewed the end of her pen.

"Did you notice Joe Berry leaving the room at all or anyone else coming in to talk to him?"

She took her time before answering. "Well, people were coming and going all the time. That Peggy woman seemed very flustered and yes, Rose was introduced to the band and came over to speak to me.

Joe did step out of the room for about ten minutes, but he was back before I went upstairs. The two guitarists seemed pre-occupied with tuning and the drummer just sat in the corner with his eyes closed. It looked to me as if he had a rough night the night before."

"What about later, after Joe had been discovered? Did you notice anything unusual?"

Cynthia raised her voice to almost a shout. "You must be joking! After Rose made that dreadful announcement everyone was in a state of shock, including me. I went back downstairs, and that Peggy woman was damn near hysterical. The band members all looked dazed and traumatised. It was Rose who seemed to take control. I cannot think of anything else to say. Can I go now?"

Susan held Cynthia back as she got up to leave the room, "Just one more thing. Could I have the name of your friend, the person who drove you from London to Bayfield?"

Cynthia's face turned red as she retorted sharply, "My friend has absolutely nothing to do with any of this."

Rose could see Susan's eyes harden. It came as no surprise when she shot back, "Ms. McArdle, this is a murder investigation. I ask the questions and expect clear answers. May I repeat myself. The name of your friend, please?"

Cynthia fidgeted her fingers and shuffled her feet before replying, "Well, if you must know he's a married man and I don't know where he lives other than the fact that his name is Mike, and he lives somewhere in London. We met on the plane. He's a sales rep on business in Ontario. We had a one-night stand, that's all."

"Right, well, at least tell me the name of the motel or hotel that you stayed in? I'll need to verify your story."

Cynthia looked shocked. "Why should I have to tell you where we stayed? It's not a police state." She looked sullen but then reluctantly decided to continue. "Oh, alright, we stayed at the Ramada Inn on Wellington and we registered under the name of Mr. and Mrs. Smith. There, I've told you and now can I leave?"

Susan had to suppress a laugh. Rose and Tom, who had tried to make themselves discreet, had overheard the whole conversation. Tom raised his eyebrows and Rose rolled her eyes. Cynthia was proving the old adage of still waters running deep...

After Cynthia had left the room Rose spoke to Susan quietly.

"You know, Susan, I distinctly got the impression that Cynthia knew Joe Berry quite well. She said something to him like, 'I haven't seen you for a long time' or something like that when I took them downstairs where she had been sitting in the room by herself. Of course, I might have misheard, but that was my impression."

Susan nodded and wrote what Rose had said in her note-book. She left soon afterwards having promised to get in touch later.

Later that morning Tom drove Cynthia to Clinton to visit with her Aunt and then drove Rose on to London to catch the mid-day Air Canada flight to Toronto, leaving just enough time to make her connecting flight to Halifax. He was back home in Bayfield by mid-afternoon and soon was snuggled up with the dogs on the sofa watching hockey.

FOUR

After Susan had breakfast with Henri, who'd arrived much later than anticipated the previous evening, she had driven to The Lion's Hall and immediately noticed the beaten up, battered Jeep that belonged to the police photographer, Peter Joyce. He was standing by the door to the building with a large brown envelope in his hand.

"Oh, I'm so glad that you're here. I was about to leave this envelope on the step for you. I have to be in Grand Bend shortly but really wanted to see you in person. I sent you the video link by the way. Did you open it?"

Susan felt a minute of guilt. She hadn't looked at her computer for almost 12 hours, Henri had been a pleasant distraction from her work, but it wasn't very professional of her and she felt a twinge of guilt.

"Thank you, Peter, so much. Do you have time for a coffee? I can put a pot on. My team won't be here for another thirty minutes or so."

Peter smiled and glanced at his watch. "I can spare thirty minutes, thank you. I would love a coffee."

They both went into the Incident room. The white board looked a little empty. Now that she had some photographs, Susan would be able to paste them to the board and write underneath the names of the key witnesses. It would look more like a proper murder case. Peter reached into the envelope and pulled out a stack of 5 x 7 glossy prints.

"I printed these off myself. These are from my old Olympus. These," he said fishing out another handful of prints, "are from the digital camera. You can see the difference?"

Susan actually couldn't see the difference, but she nodded and went along with it because this was obviously something that Peter took quite seriously. She quietly observed the man as he went through each photograph. He was about six foot tall, loose limbed, and athletic looking in a lean, rugged way. He reminded her of an Australian outbacker, not that she knew such a man, but on television she had seen the type. A man's man is how she would describe him, like the Formula 1 drivers whom she found really attractive and very masculine. He had kind eyes that seemed incongruous in such a tough looking man. She wondered if he was married or, indeed, what was his story?

"Here you are," she said handing him a steaming mug of coffee.

"So, Peter, how long have you lived around these parts?" Susan hadn't a clue whether he lived in Bayfield or Goderich, but she was dying to find out.

"Actually, I live in London, but I am a freelance photographer specializing in police work. I used to work for National Geographic in my past life, but now I do as little or as much work as I care to and love it."

"That makes two of us then, I mean, both of us living in London. I'm pretty close to retirement but I'm not sure yet if I'll be able to cope with doing nothing."

"A few years ago, I officially retired from working for the National Geographic. My life was turned upside down by a turn of events and I felt that I couldn't function any more at the high pace required of a top magazine photographer. For a year I wallowed in self-pity and then I got up, picked up the pieces of my life, and started photographing again. The rest is history. I work every now and then when I'm called in, but the rest of the time I photograph wildlife, mostly birds and am finally at peace with the world."

"Boy, that's some story. Where do you live in London?"

"I live just opposite Spring Bank Gardens. It's an ideal spot for photographing birds. In fact, it's a beautiful park altogether. I tell you what, I'll give you my business card and next time you're in London look me up. I would love to show you some of my work."

Peter handed Susan a black and gold card with *Black Gold Photography* printed in bold print. She took it from him and tucked it into her black wallet. She waved to the handsome photographer who had come into her life just like the wind. *You never knew what was around the corner,* Susan thought as she watched Peter Joyce drive away in his old Jeep.

TOM WOKE UP WITH A START. Had it all been a dreadful nightmare or had Gillian Jeffries actually tried, and almost succeeded, in seducing him? His thoughts whirled around his head as he recounted the previous evening. He had driven first Cynthia to Clinton and then Rose to London airport. He had returned to an empty house, well, not exactly empty as Ben and Puff were always present, but without Rose somehow their home lost its soul and Tom suddenly felt excessively lonely.

. . .

AFTER SPENDING an hour clearing the snow and then making sure that he had put the shepherd's pie that Rose had made for him, in the oven, he opened a beer and was just sitting down to watch the hockey, when the doorbell rang. It was Gillian Jeffries.

"Oh Tom, Tom, can I come in?" Without waiting for an answer, she stepped inside and shrugged off her coat and boots. Turning to Tom he could see her beautiful eyes start to overflow with glistening tears. She stumbled over to him and wrapped her arms around him crying softly in his ear.

"Tom, I can't get the picture of Joe Berry dead on the floor out of my mind. I can't, I can't…"

Her whole body began to convulse with emotion.

Tom pulled her to him and kissed her wet cheeks and before he knew what had happened Gillian was grabbing at his shirt, pulling off the buttons, kissing his exposed chest, and undoing the zip in his pants. Tom could not, would not, resist the urge to run his hands down her silky back, feel the hardness of her breasts pressing so close against his body which now felt so alive and tingling with desire. Gillian started to lick his neck, his chest, tried to pull down his pants, and was about to remove his briefs when the phone rang.

"Ignore it," Gillian whispered huskily, "I need you. I want you, oh Tom, take me now."

But Tom had never been able to ignore the phone. Many of his friends never answered the phone, always leaving it to go to messages, but not Tom. Besides, he knew exactly who was calling. It would be Rose. He gently pushed Gillian away and almost tripped on his own pants which had fallen down around his ankles. He hopped over to the phone grabbing it quickly before it stopped ringing.

"Oh, hi Tom, my love. You sound all out of breath. Is everything okay?"

Tom took a big gulp of air and tried to steady his shaking voice. Out of the corner of his eye he saw Gillian disappear off into his bedroom.

"Oh, Rose, I miss you so much." He had to stop himself from crying. What had he been about to do? Was he crazy?

"Tom, my darling, you do sound strange. But I've got to tell you, Oliver is the spitting image of you. He looks like a miniature Grandpa. Oh, he is so adorable, and Anne and Alan are positively walking on air. I'm so happy for them, but I miss you too!"

Tom felt a lump form in his throat. He couldn't talk, he could barely breathe. Finally, he whispered, "Rose, I love you." And put down the phone while wiping away the tears rolling down his cheeks. He pulled up his pants, grabbed his shirt, and was about to put it on when Gillian appeared absolutely stark naked.

Tom just stood there and couldn't help but soak up the magnificent body before him. Gillian was so toned that she didn't have an inch of spare fat on her. She looked like a Greek Goddess. Tom felt his resistance waver. His whole body craved the wanton woman before him, but no, he had to be strong.

"Gillian, you are a beautiful and a desirable woman, but I am a happily married man. Now put your clothes on. You must leave now before I do something that I'll live to regret."

"But Tom, I just know that you want me. For the past three months you've flirted outrageously with me at the gym. Now come on. Nobody needs to tell Rose. Look, I'm offering you my body. Take me."

Tom turned his head away, averted his eyes and moved away from the temptress.

"Gillian, you must leave now." With that he went to the bedroom, picked up her clothes and threw them at her.

She grabbed them and almost snarled as she shouted.

"This is your last chance, Tom. I never offer myself twice. Oh, go to hell!" She quickly pulled on her clothes, grabbed her winter coat and boots and rushed out of the house.

Tom smelt the shepherd's pie burning as he rushed to take it out of the oven.

SUSAN STIFLED A YAWN. It had been a long night, admittedly an amazingly wonderful night, but she definitely felt sleep deprived that morning. She looked around at her motley team. They really could do with more bodies.

Investigating a murder took up so many man hours. Just trying to make do with four officers was almost ridiculous. Cost cutting. It was always about the budget.

Pouring out her second cup of coffee she took a sip, grimaced and then called the room to order.

"Good morning, everyone. I have just received the preliminary forensic report. The victim died of massive blood loss. The main jugular vein had been severed. He would have died within minutes. According to the report the knife blade was ten inches long. The attack took place from behind, although forensics believe that the murderer approached the victim and swung him around to stab him. Alternatively, the knife could have been drawn while in a hugging position. Whatever, evidence suggests that the perpetrator knew the victim.

There were no signs of a struggle. There was evidence of the victim attempting to remove the knife from his neck. In fact, he died clutching the knife handle. Also, the toxicology report states that there was a high level of narcotics in his blood, cocaine. Any questions?"

Constable Brown put up his hand. "Ma'am, could forensics tell whether the velocity of the thrust of the knife could have been inflicted by either male or female?"

Susan looked up from her notes. "That is a good question. I've just scanned the report and it appears that the degree of force required to thrust the knife deeply into the neck would certainly require a strong arm. There is no mention of gender specific. Constable, come here, and let's conduct a demonstration."

Susan found a ruler and approached the Constable with the 'weapon' behind her back. Suddenly she grabbed his shoulders, and with the speed of lightning she arched her ruler around to the back of his neck at the same time as pulling him towards her.

"Voila," she said smiling at the shocked face of Constable Brown. "So, you see, it could be executed by a woman, in fact, it's all about the level of surprise and the speed of the attack. Okay, let's move on to our reports. Sergeant Flowers, you interviewed the band members. What did you learn?"

The Sergeant stood up, shuffled his notes, cleared his throat, and proceeded to read from them.

"The bass guitarist, Bill Jenson, has been with the band since its inception in 1968. Joe Berry and Bill went to High School together and started playing in Joe's garage way back in 1967 when they were both sixteen-year-olds. Bill appeared genuinely shaken by Joe's death and could barely speak as he was so choked up with emotion. The drummer, on the other hand, a John Selbrook, only joined the group five years ago after they had got back together and seemed quite nonplussed by it all."

Susan interrupted the Sergeant. "You mean to say that The Berries had disbanded. When and why?"

"Well, it appeared that they had a falling out way back in the eighties. Bill was a bit vague about the details. The other guitarist, Adam Frank, was even vaguer about what happened, but he mentioned some woman's name, Patricia, and Joe Berries wife, Jenny."

Susan once more interrupted Sergeant Flowers. "So, let me get this straight. The Berries were formed in 1968 with Bill and Joe being the founding members. If they broke up in the 80's that means that they were together as a band for almost fifteen years. What happened to the original drummer and lead guitarist?"

Sergeant Flowers looked embarrassed. He stammered as he spoke. "Well, ma'am, Bill was very vague, and Adam was just nonchalant. He, too, had only joined the group later on when they had re-formed. By then they were already a big name, so he came riding in on their cloak of fame. It does sound as if Joe Berry was a bit of as ladies' man. He seemed to have had groupies in each city. I went online and found The Berries fan club. It appears that Joe had quite the following, mostly women. Unfortunately, computers were not around at the peak of their popularity."

Susan thought for a minute before saying, "Go through the fan list again, Sergeant, and see if you can find any familiar names. Have you anything further to add?"

"No, ma'am. I was going to follow up my inquiries with Joe Berries wife, Jenny. I was also going to see if I could find out who this Patricia woman is and try to track down the original band members?" He sat down and put his notebook away.

"Thank you, Sergeant. Now, Constables Brown and

Elliot, how are you getting on with interviewing the audience from the concert?"

The two Constables stood up and flicked through their notes. Constable Brown spoke first.

"A Ron Jones of Cameron Street sat next to The Berries at The Albion. He reckoned that there was some bad blood between the drummer and Joe Berry. They seemed to be having an argument, but he couldn't make out what was being said. A Linda Walsh substantiated this. She was also having dinner at The Albion and witnessed the men arguing. She thought that the bass guitarist, Bill, was part of the problem. Oh, and this Ron said that Joe was on his cell phone for quite a while during their meal. Everybody else on my list appeared genuinely sorry and shocked about the murder. They were all fans of The Berries."

Constable Elliot interjected. "There was one woman, a Gillian Jeffries, who openly sobbed when we contacted her on the phone. She said that she had known him before he was famous. Everyone else seemed really shocked by the turn of events. That's all, ma'am."

"Okay, thank you, men. Now who was supposed to have interviewed this Gillian Jeffries? I see that she was reported to have had an argument with the deceased not long before he was murdered. In fact, she might have been the last person to have seen him alive."

Constable Mathieson stood up.

"Ma'am, I attempted to interview her. In fact, I waited for her to turn up for over thirty minutes yesterday, but she never showed up. She owns, A Time for Toning, and I had arranged to meet her there yesterday at 9:00 a.m. She did a no show and then I got busy with interviewing the rest of the group. I'll try again later on today."

"Good," Susan said and then continued talking, "I interviewed the chairperson of the Town Hall Committee, Peggy Grierson. She found the body. The murder weapon, the knife, was purchased at a kitchen shop in Goderich called 'Kulpeppers', and it was part of a set that Rose Blair purchased for $80. The fact that it was a knife taken from the kitchen, tells me that the murderer must have been familiar with the kitchen at the Town Hall. This in turn indicates to me that our perpetrator could be someone local from the community with inside knowledge of the kitchen."

Sergeant Mathieson stood up. "Not necessarily, ma'am. The harpist and the band members were all downstairs for a good hour sitting in the meeting room adjacent to the kitchen. Any one of them could have access to the knives in the drawer."

Susan's face blushed as she felt somewhat challenged by her Sergeant's tone. Of course, what he had said made perfect sense, but it also made a bit of a mockery of her statement.

"Well, it does narrow our search down somewhat. I interviewed the harpist, Cynthia McArdle. She seemed very adept at telling lies and was almost aggressive when I asked about her personal life. I feel that she has something to hide. I would definitely categorize her as a person of interest. To sum up, there was obviously some bad blood between the band members, Gillian Jeffries also had an argument with Joe Berry shortly before he was killed.

As to Cynthia McArdle, she is hiding something. She claims not to have known The Berries, but I suspect otherwise. We need to interview these two women. Sergeant, can you deal with this today? Constables Brown and Elliot, go and speak to the band members again and also interview their respective partners, wives, children, and parents. I need to have a complete picture of what Joe was like and what possible motive there would be to have him murdered. Right, go to it men, and bring me back some results."

Susan looked at her watch. She'd arranged to meet Henri at The Little Inn for lunch and had thirty minutes to spare. Time enough to pop into the village book shop. It was Henri's birthday next week and she knew exactly what he would like as a present.

ROSE ARRIVED in Halifax the previous evening exactly on schedule. Alan was at the airport to meet her, and Anne was already home from the hospital. Alan had driven them over the Angus McDonald Bridge across to Dartmouth. Turning left onto Pine Street, he told Rose that the Common was very close by. In the summer, Rose thought, Anne would be able to take Oliver for some lovely walks in the park.

They pulled up outside a small, red bricked bungalow. There was a neat patch of what would be grass but was now just a snowy square surrounded by dwarf pine trees. A yellow wrought iron gate led up a recently shovelled pathway. The front door was painted a bright red and suddenly burst opened. Anne ran out with her arms flung wide.

"Mum, it's wonderful to see you." She hugged Rose and pulled her inside. Alan followed carrying Rose's small suitcase.

"So, where is my grandson?" Rose laughed as she looked around the messy living room and kitchen. Anne had never been able to keep a tidy room, let alone a house. What she lacked in tidiness though, she made up with warmth.

"He's sound asleep, Mom, but come into his room and you can see him."

Rose followed Anne into a small box room painted a fresh lemon yellow. Orange ducks had been stencilled around the walls and an orange and white fluffy rug rested on the pine boarded floor. There, lying in a white crib, lay the dearest little baby with a shock of black hair and a cherubic face.

"Oh, he's just beautiful, darling." Rose whispered, "Just so perfect in every way. He looks just like you did as a baby."

"Mom, I think that he looks just like Alan."

Love is blind, Rose thought as she took in all the details of her new grandson. Tiny, pink shell-like ears and such cherubic rosebud lips, he didn't look in the least bit like his father, Alan who, although quite good looking, had a beak of a nose and rather coarse features.

"Is he feeding alright, my love?" Rose asked remembering how difficult a perfectly natural act like breast feeding had turned into a nightmare for her as a new mother all those years ago. It had taken over two weeks to finally get into a proper routine of feeding Jessica.

Just then Oliver let out a little whimper. His mouth twitched and then his whole body squirmed as he woke up. Opening his startling, inky blue eyes, he looked up at his grandma and then let out an almighty cry. Anne reacted instantly and scooped up the precious bundle, taking him over to a little rocking chair over by the bedroom window.

Rose watched mesmerized as Anne expertly latched the baby on and gently rocked him gently to and fro as he gulped down his feed. She almost felt embarrassed to be part of the very intimate moment between mother and child.

ROSE HAD RISEN early and gone downstairs into the messy kitchen. She filled up the kettle and then put some hot, soapy, water in the sink. Rolling up her sweater sleeves, she proceeded to wash all the dirty dishes and tidied up the kitchen. She opened the fridge to see how well stocked it was. Looking at a few shrivelled up carrots, two yoghurts, one mouldy apple, and a dried lump of cheese, Rose decided shopping would be high on her list of priorities. She had just finished drying the last of the washing up when Anne appeared carrying Oliver.

"Here you are, Mom. I thought you might like to have a cuddle." She handed Oliver over to Rose who cradled the little darling tightly in her arms.

"Oh, love, he is so precious." She stroked his velvety, soft skin and looked at the little miracle of life before her. Tears welled up in Rose's eyes.

"Mom, why are you crying?" Anne asked looking startled at her mother.

Rose wiped her eyes and smiled at her daughter. "Darling, I'm just feeling overwhelmed by Oliver's perfection. Sorry, my love. Excuse your sentimental, old mother. New babies always make me cry."

Anne smiled and gave Rose a hug. "I do feel blessed, Mom. I can't keep my eyes off him. I love him so much."

Alan came into the kitchen and joined the women. The kettle had just come to a boil and Alan deftly made a pot of tea and put on some toast.

He poured out the tea and they sat down at the kitchen table which Rose had earlier cleared and covered with a clean tablecloth and placemats that she had found in the dresser drawers.

"Did you sleep alright, Rose?" Alan asked as he put the cups of tea down onto the table.

In truth Rose had slept badly. The hastily made-up single bed in the spare room was most uncomfortable and Rose had found herself awake half of the night. She smiled and said, "I slept okay, but after breakfast I would like to go and do some shopping. Where is the nearest supermarket?"

"I'll take you," Alan said, "We can leave Anne and Oliver to rest."

Rose finished her tea and toast and prepared to go out into the cold. Nova Scotia felt quite damp compared to Ontario and there wasn't as much snow although there was a bitterly cold Atlantic wind which chilled Rose to her bones.

Alan drove down to the end of the street and it was then that Rose noticed the sign for Myrtle Street. *Cynthia McArdle lives down there,* she thought as they turned the corner.

She noticed a small convenience store and made a mental note that if they ran out of anything it would be an easy walk to the shop from Alan and Anne's house. It took ten minutes to get to the supermarket.

ROSE WALKED UP and down the aisles with Alan filling up the shopping cart finally ending up with some large and expensive packets of baby diapers.

Rose recalled the chore of washing cloth nappies when Jessica was a baby. By the time that Paul came along, disposable diapers were available, but she only used them when they were travelling. They were in those days so horribly expensive. At least her old cloth diapers were re-useable. It was a disposable world now and convenience was the key to modern living.

After they returned from shopping Rose made them all some lunch and spent a glorious afternoon getting to know her new grandson.

FIVE

The next day Rose got up early and saw Alan off to work. She set to baking. First, she made some scrambled eggs on toast for Anne, poured out some fresh orange juice, and made a pot of tea. She carried this all on a tray to Anne's bedroom and set it down on the bedside table. Anne was busy feeding Oliver. She looked up when she saw Rose and said, "Mom, you don't have to wait on me. I'm not an invalid, but thanks all the same. Come and say hallo to your grandson."

Rose bent over and gave him a little kiss. "I'm going to leave you now, love, to do some cooking. Try to get a nap in when you've finished feeding Oliver." With that Rose left the bedroom and went back to the kitchen. She was determined to stock the fridge and freezer with ready-made meals for Anne and Alan. She would also make a whole load of cookies and scones.

She got busy and soon was lost in the world of baking. By the end of the morning, she had made three different soups, two lasagnes, three shepherd's pies, and a large beef casserole.

Anne was amazed at the quantity of food her mother had produced.

"I've run out of milk," Rose declared to Anne. "I'll just walk to the convenience store and pick some up." With that she put on her thick winter coat and boots and grabbing her purse, Rose set off down the road.

When she got to the convenience store, she looked around but could not see the proprietor anywhere. Taking a sack of milk out of the fridge, Rose went over to the counter. She had been wrong. The owner of the shop had been there all along. She was sitting in a comfortable armchair down behind the counter watching a small television. She must have been in her late eighties, but from her keen expression Rose could see that she was a very spry octogenarian.

"How can I help you, my lass? You look new around here."

Rose smiled. "Yes, I'm visiting my daughter and son-in-law who live just around the corner. They have just had a new baby and I'm down for a few days to help."

"Oh, yes, I had heard they had a new wee one. They're both professors at the university, aren't they?"

Rose nodded. This busy body would know everybody and everyone's business she thought, and then, after a pause while the old lady rang the milk into the till and took her debit card, Rose said "Do you know the McArdle's of Myrtle Street?"

The old woman's mouth pursed into a hard grimace.

"I most certainly do or should I say did. The McArdle's were good friends of mine. First Eric died and then shortly afterwards his wife passed away leaving that snotty nosed daughter, Cynthia, to inherit everything. Oh my, I could tell you a thing or two about that."

Rose thought, *please do*, but she just stood there quietly

waiting for the old lady to continue. Sometimes just remaining silent was the best tactic when wanting someone to talk.

"Yes, you see, she was trouble with a capital T right from when she got knocked up at university by that fellow. You know, the one that got himself killed. I read about it in the papers. He was in a band, the apples or cherries or something like that. She followed him everywhere, even though he made it pretty clear that he didn't want her. He even had to take out a restraining order on her.

Then she got tied up with the drug scene in Montreal. She led her poor parents a real song and dance. Spoilt she was and what thanks did she ever give them for everything that they did for her?

Mind, she plays the harp beautifully and now that she's settled down, seems normal, but she's a strange one that Cynthia."

Rose couldn't wait to get home so that she could phone Tom and give him the scoop. Susan should know as soon as possible too. Serendipity came to Rose's mind as she walked back to Pine Street. Life was just one massive web of connec-tions just waiting to come together.

HENRI LEFT Bayfield early that morning but not before Susan and he had made sweet, tender love. The two days they had spent together had been just the right tonic needed for both of them even though their time together had been fragmented with the murder inquiry.

Over dinner the previous day they had actually talked about their future together. Tentative plans had been made and Susan felt that the future looked good. Parting was always such a sweet sorrow, but they had arranged to meet up again in two weeks. In the meantime, Susan and her team had a murder to solve.

AFTER A REFRESHING SWIM in the indoor pool of The Bayfield Village Inn, Susan drove to The Lion's Hall. She smelt the coffee immediately before she opened the door.

On the table was a tray of Bicycle Shop take out coffee. The owners of the shop roasted their own beans and sold the most delicious freshly brewed coffee from their shop. Today's brew was from Guatemala.

"Good morning, everyone. I hope that you have something new for me because this case is beginning to slow down, and we have to up the momentum. Right, Constable Mathieson, what have you to report?"

The Constable stood up looking a bit awkward. He shuffled his pages around and then coughed as he cleared his throat.

"Well, ma'am, the fitness instructor, Gillian Jeffries, has eluded me completely. I went around to A Time for Toning yesterday and she hadn't turned up all day. I drove to her house and there was no sign of her there either. I will go back again today. As to Cynthia, I went around to the Blair's where she was staying.

There was only Tom Blair in the house. He said Cynthia McArdle had gone to visit an aunt in Clinton on Sunday before flying home to Nova Scotia.

He had actually dropped her off at her aunt's house before driving to London where he was taking his wife to catch a plane to Halifax.

I got the aunt's address and telephone number from him but so far, I've had no success in getting a hold of either the aunt or Cynthia. I'll like to catch her before she heads out to

Halifax so maybe I might strike lucky this afternoon. That's all I have to report, ma'am."

"Okay, Constables Brown and Elliot, what have you to report? Please tell me something positive."

The two Constables stood up. Brown took the lead.

"Bill Jenson, the bass guitarist and co-founder of the group, revealed quite a lot when we interviewed him again. He was married to Patricia, who left him for Joe Berry. That caused a major split in the band.

When Joe wanted to get The Berries back on tour, Bill and he had a big reconciliation. The drummer, John Selbrook, has only been with the band for five years but he had known Bill Jenson for a long time before he joined the band.

He told me that after Patricia left, Bill went on a complete bender. For years he became a binge drinker, was unemployed, and was generally at rock bottom until he met Cynthia McArdle."

Susan interrupted Constable Brown, "You said Cynthia. Do you mean our Cynthia McArdle? She flatly denied knowing anyone in the band. How many years ago was this?"

The Constable flicked through his notes. "Umm…let me see. It was six years after the band split up which would have been around 1994. According to John, Cynthia and Bill were together for about five years."

"Thank you, Constable. What about the lead guitarist, Adam Frank?"

Constable Elliot stood up and opened his notebook. He cleared his throat before speaking.

"Adam Frank only joined the band when they regrouped five years ago. Before that he was with The Starbursts out of Winnipeg. He had never met Joe Berry in person before joining the group. He said that The Berries were before his time as he is only thirty-four. He said that his parents were fans and they had been quite tickled when they heard that he had joined the group.

Adam is still amazed at the popularity of the band. He said that every gig they played has been to full houses. It was also apparent that Joe Berry had been the main draw.

He apparently attracted women like a magnet. According to Adam, Joe was a right womanizer. He fancied himself with the ladies."

Susan interrupted the Constable again. "Did Adam or indeed any of the other band members overhear the argument between Joe and Gillian Jeffries?"

Constable Elliot continued. "Ma'am, it was never confirmed that what Tom actually heard was in fact Joe Berry and Gillian Jeffries. We don't know conclusively who it was arguing. Adam did say that he had heard raised voices. He actually thought that it was the harpist shouting as she had left the room."

Susan interrupted again. "I thought Cynthia said she had not left the room?"

Constable Elliot began to look a little irritated by all the interruptions, but he regained his composure and continued. "According to both Adam and Bill, Cynthia left the room several times. She may have just gone to the washroom, but she could just as easily have gone into the kitchen and procured the knife. However, she couldn't have stabbed our victim as she was on stage at the time of the murder. That's all I have to report ma'am."

"Thank you, Constable. Well, men, it does seem imperative that we interview both Gillian Jeffries and Cynthia McArdle.

Sergeant Flowers, I would like you to go with Constable Mathieson around to Ms. Jeffries house. Constables Brown and Elliot you need to try to get hold of Cynthia McArdle. I would also like you to interview the deceased's wife, Jenny. I believe that all of these women hold the key to unlocking the motive for murder. Now we need to expedite this carefully. We will meet tomorrow at 8:00 a.m. I cannot stress how important it is to get results. Go to it team."

Susan sat still, deep in contemplation. Joe Berry was obviously a philandering, womaniser and had probably always been that way. His wife, Jenny, would in all probability reveal as much about the man.

Henri Le Bruin flashed through her mind as if the two were somehow connected. Susan wasn't sure if she could totally trust Henri. He was, after all, a good-looking man and she knew very little about him.

She had never felt the desire to probe into his past. She did that daily with other people's lives. It somehow felt a profanity of their relationship to even be contemplating running a search on the man she loved.

But she had been taken in once before by another handsome man, Jim Reynolds. He had reeled her in hook, line, and sinker, and in his case, she had known that he was a married man. His wheeling and dealing in the underworld had, however, completely eluded her. As if reading her mind Susan's cell phone rang. It was indeed her fiancé, Henri Le Bruin.

"*Ma Cherie*, I have some urgent news. Interpol has just contacted us. Jim Reynold's is on his way to Canada. Cherie, I worry about you. This man is dangerous. You must promise me to be on the lookout for him. He has become the master of disguise so be warned. We think that he will try to make contact with his family in Wingham. That is less than an hour away from Bayfield. Just be careful, *ma Cherie*."

"Does his family know that he is on his way to Canada?"

There was a slight pause as Henri prepared to speak. "No. They do not know, but we have them under twenty four hour surveillance."

"But what about you Henri? Do you not think that he might go after you?"

Susan's voice had taken on an edge. She was not worried about herself. Jim would never harm her, but he had not shied away from killing three times in Bayfield. He was a ruthless man on the run and if cornered like a wild animal, he would stop at nothing.

BACK IN DARTMOUTH, Rose spent the rest of the day inside the house helping Anne get used to feeding little Oliver and generally trying to boost her morale. After all the euphoria of giving birth, Anne had crashed into a typical baby blues depression.

She complained to her mother that she still looked about six months pregnant, that her hair was so greasy she looked such a mess, and so it went on.

Rose did her best to reassure her daughter that all of this was perfectly normal, that her figure would return really quickly with breastfeeding, and that her hair was just greasy because of the surge of hormones rushing through her body. Oliver on the other hand, seemed as content as a kitten.

He gulped milk from his mother with such gusto that Rose feared he would choke. His little fists curled up as his head nestled against the warmth of Anne's body and he made little mewling sounds as he took his feed. Rose had made it her job to burp the baby, so after each feed she had whisked Oliver away from Anne and told her to go and get some rest.

Rose then spent a pleasant half hour rubbing the baby's back and holding him over her shoulder while she rocked him to and fro. It was amazing how one never forgot how to hold a baby and to generally take care of a newborn. It was like second nature and it was so much easier when it was not your own baby.

Rose remembered her own sleepless nights pacing up and down with a colicky baby screaming, knees bent, little face red and scrunched up in pain. Jessica had been the colicky one and had caused more sleepless nights than the other two put together.

Of course, she had also been her first baby and it had all been terrifyingly new to Tom and her, parenthood that is. It should have been the most natural thing in the world having and raising a baby, but the responsibility and care of that little scrap of humanity born of such love was mind boggling to the young Rose.

However did I manage, she thought as Oliver started to cry and root around for more milk. Babies changed your life irrevocably and wonderfully and no one would ever have believed the extent until they entered into parenthood themselves. Anne and Alan had only just begun their journey of discovery.

"He is so adorable, darling, absolutely perfect in every way," Rose kept saying. She couldn't stop looking at her little grandson. He truly was perfection personified.

As this was Rose's last day in Halifax, Alan offered to take Rose on a little sightseeing trip while Anne and Oliver slept. Alan insisted on showing Rose around the university saying that she couldn't possibly travel all this way without seeing where they worked. Actually, Rose would have been just as happy staying inside as the cold Atlantic wind was biting, and the sea was not at all inviting.

Everything seemed muted in fog and her impression of the city was one of greyness and cold. Alan was proud of the observatory in his department. Being an astrophysicist meant he had a real affinity with the stars.

Rose feigned interest in black holes and dark galaxies and had to stifle a big yawn as Alan lectured her with an obvious passion in his subject. After their visit to Dalhousie, Alan drove her around the city centre, and once again, started to lecture Rose on the history of Halifax.

Apparently, the town of Halifax was named after the British Earl of Halifax and was founded in 1749. She also learned that the Sambro Lighthouse was the oldest lighthouse in the whole of North America and dated back to 1758. British forts were erected, namely the Citadel in Halifax, to protect the British colonials from the French, Mi'kmaq, and Arcadians.

Rose also learned about one of the modern-day disasters in Halifax that took place in 1917 during the First World War.

The SS Mont-Blanc, a French cargo ship carrying munitions for the war, collided with a Belgium Relief vessel, the SS AImo, resulting in an explosion which devastated the whole Richmond district of Halifax, killing over two thou- sand people and injuring nearly nine thousand others.

This was the largest blast of an artificial substance ever known to man before the development of nuclear weapons.

After the tour and the history lesson, Rose was thoroughly exhausted. She liked Alan, but he was somewhat dry and slightly pompous, particularly when he lectured to her for hours. Finally, he drove them back to the cosy, little house on Pine Street, which Rose was beginning to call home.

As soon as they entered the house, they could hear the melodious wailing of a colicky baby. Rose rushed in and took Oliver from Anne who was looking distinctly tearful and extremely tired.

"Mom, I don't think I can do this."

"Of course, you will manage, darling. Just try to relax and you'll be fine. Look, he's stopped crying now. Try him with some more milk and he'll probably go straight to sleep. The little thing is, no doubt, exhausted after his screaming session."

Poor Anne, Rose thought. She had a tough time ahead of her as all new mothers have to face. She will just have to get through it, and she hoped that Anne had a good support system of close friends who would help her over the first few weeks while she established her routine.

Rose wished she lived closer so that she could be of more help to her daughter now when she needed it the most.

SIX

Snow fell in big, wet flakes which Tom feared might turn to ice. He was on his way to London to pick Rose up from the airport. Driving to London in the winter always put him on edge as the weather could be so unpredictable. Tom glanced at his watch. It was 11:00 a.m. and Rose's flight was due in at mid-day.

It felt as if she had been gone far longer than the three days. So much had happened in that short time, although, from what he had heard, really not much progress had been made on the murder case. Tom reigned his thoughts in case they should dwell on Gillian Jeffries and his near infidelity. His chest still constricted every time that he remembered the events of that first evening after Rose had left. He had not seen Gillian since, indeed, he had purposely kept away from Time for Toning, although Doug said that absolutely no one from the village had seen her or heard from her for the past three days.

The police, he knew, wanted to interview her regarding the murder at the Town Hall. Thinking about the Town Hall,

Tom tried to recall the argument that he overheard around the time of the murder. At the time he had been convinced that it was Gillian Jeffries arguing with a man, but could it have been some other woman?

Maybe he had only thought it was her because he had seen her hovering around the basement just prior to the argument. All these thoughts and others rushed through Tom's head so much so that he almost rear-ended a car turning left in the hamlet of Arva. He finally pulled into the airport parking lot with ten minutes to spare. Time enough to pick up two coffees from Tim Horton's, one for Rose and one for him.

THE PASSENGERS CAME CROWDING through the arrivals door and then Tom saw her, his darling Rose, looking delightfully flushed, half pulling, half dragging her bright red carry-on case. She waved at Tom and blew him a kiss as she finally, in exasperation, picked up the suitcase and carried it in her arms.

Her cheeks were pink, and her eyes sparkled. She wore a new emerald green winter jacket and on her head, she wore a black woollen beret. Wisps of golden hair fluffed up around the soft wool of her hat.

"Oh, Tom, one of the wheels of my case dropped off." Rose exclaimed as she reached him and then they were in each other's arms and Tom kissed her on her lips, a warm, lingering kiss. He squeezed her shoulders and with a gruff, thick voice, said, "Rose, I missed you more than you will ever know."

.   .   .

THEY DROVE BACK to Bayfield with Rose talking nonstop about Anne, Alan, and darling baby Oliver.

Finally, she got on to the subject of Cynthia McArdle.

"Well, Tom, I can hardly wait to tell Susan about Cynthia's relationship with Joe Berry. She practically stalked the man for years. I would say that she should be their prime suspect, don't you think?"

Tom was tired. All he wanted to do was to forget everything about the murder.

"Give it a rest, Rose. Just promise me that you're not going to get involved with all of this. Look, pass on the information to Susan and then leave it to her, please, my love."

They had pulled up into their driveway. The house looked particularly charming blanketed in snow, just like a gingerbread house. Rose could hear Ben and Puff barking with excitement at her homecoming. It was so good to be home, Rose thought as she opened the front door and was greeted effusively by her darling dogs.

SUSAN ARRIVED at the Lion's Hall early. She filled up the coffee maker with water and spooned coffee grounds into the filter. Her mind still dwelled on her conversation with Henri and the disconcerting fact that Jim Reynolds was likely back in Canada.

He had been out of sight and out of mind for two years. Why would he risk everything to return? She thought about his wife and children. Could they have been in touch with him these past few years? She shook her head in an effort to clear her thoughts. *Focus on the case*, she told herself as she glanced at the photographs of Joe Berry lying dead in the tiny jail of the Town Hall. The case was progressing at such a snail's pace. She hoped today's meeting would yield some much-needed information.

HER TEAM STARTED to trickle in. First Sergeant Flowers arrived looking suitably glum. He was a good-looking officer in a rugged way, but his looks would be greatly enhanced if the man would smile more often, Susan thought. Constable Mathieson appeared next and in contrast to the Sergeant, he always looked dapper and more often than not wore a big, chirpy smile on his face.

"Good morning, ma'am." He called out. "Is it cold enough for you?"

The morning's temperature had read -22 degrees. The winter showed no sign of letting up. Mind you, February, in Susan's mind, was always the coldest month of the year. It was just a case of holding in and waiting until March when the beginnings of Spring would start to be seen.

Constables Brown and Elliot arrived.

"Right men." Susan said, impatient to start the briefing. "Firstly, I have the full report from forensics. I'll read out the relevant section. The cut across the victim's throat fully trans-acted the left jugular vein, severing the left carotid artery and nicking the right jugular. Three inches at its deepest, the knife cut into the spinal column. The report suggests that a large, single edged knife was used as the weapon."

Susan put the report down and looked around the room.

"No real surprises there, but it is consistent with what we know. Joe was stabbed to death with a kitchen knife. So, let's have your reports.

Sergeant Flowers and Constable Mathieson what have you to say. How did you make out with Cynthia McArdle and Gillian Jeffries?"

Sergeant Flowers coughed and looked down at his feet before answering, "Well… Cynthia McArdle had already flown back to Halifax. We tried to reach her by telephone, but she doesn't answer our calls. We will keep trying. As for Gillian Jeffries, well, we went around again to her house and knocked on the door but still no answer. We wondered, ma'am, if we have permission to break the door down to enter?"

Susan felt exasperated. Two key witnesses and still they had not managed to interview either one.

"Yes, go ahead. Try to break in as discreetly as possible. If she has gone away and returns to find a smashed in door we will be in trouble. Okay, I need to hear some good news. Constables Brown and Elliot, how did you make out with our victim's wife?"

Both Constables stood up in unison. They looked at each other as if to gauge who would speak first. Susan was in no mood for games.

"Well, come on, one of you talk. Constable Brown, you go ahead."

The Constable opened his notebook and proceeded to read from his notes.

"We interviewed Jenny Berry at her home on Windsor Drive, Roncesvalles in Toronto. Joe Berry not only leaves a grieving widow but three children, two daughters, Vivien and Scarlet and a son, Eric.

For all intent and purpose, according to Jenny, they were happily married. She laughed when I mentioned other women. He apparently has a whole entourage of female groupies. She showed me some of his fan letters and sure enough there were enough declarations of undying love to fill this room."

Susan interrupted the constable abruptly, "Wasn't there a

woman called Patricia involved with Joe and wasn't she the original cause of the split up of the group?"

"Yes, ma'am, Bill Jenson, the bass guitarist was married to Patricia in the early days of The Berries. This was before Joe met Jenny. Well, according to Bill, Joe stole his wife, and they had a massive argument resulting in Joe and Bill going their separate ways. Joe and Patricia stayed together for a few years and then they split up."

"Did Jenny know anything about this or was it ancient history by the time she met Joe?"

"Jenny said that she heard about the split, but Patricia had been out of the picture for at least a year before Joe and she got together."

Susan interrupted the Constable again.

"Did you track down Patricia? What is her full name anyway?"

Constable Elliot stepped forward and, opening his notebook, took the lead.

"Her full name is Patricia Anne Walker and yes, ma'am, we did track her down. Unfortunately, records show that she now lives in New Zealand and has been married for thirty-five years. She has five children. They live in Christchurch."

"Right, well, that rules her out. Thank you, men. So that still leaves us with our two prime suspects, Cynthia and Gillian. Hopefully between them, they'll be able to fill in the missing pieces.

Now, we do also have Bill Jenson who might have been still harbouring a grudge. After all, he did start up the group all those years ago with Joe and then had his wife stolen from him. I think that I will pay Bill Jenson a visit myself.

In the meantime, can the two of you track down Gillian Jeffries and try to get hold of Cynthia McArdle, even if it means involving the Halifax police?

We'll meet the same time tomorrow. Go to it, men and bring me back some results."

The men vacated the room leaving Susan deep in thought. Thoughts of Jim Reynolds kept drifting in and out. The man had always had a way of getting under her skin but this time she did not tingle with excitement at the thought of seeing him. Instead, her skin cringed and the hairs on her arms stood on end.

If she was truthful to herself, she would admit to being really frightened.

AFTER THE INITIAL excitement of returning home and being greeted so wonderfully by Tom, Ben, and Puff, Rose got around to tidying up. She had only been away for three days but already the house looked like a storm had hit it.

Tom was normally quite good at keeping on top of the housework but this time it looked as if he had totally abandoned everything. Dishes had been left piled up in the sink. A half-eaten and rather burnt shepherd's pie had been left out on the dining room table, rumpled clothes were strewn across the floor in the bedroom, and so it went on. She didn't say a word to Tom, just knuckled down to tidying up. When she had finished, she let out a deep sigh.

"Tom, I'm really tired. Do you think you could make us both a pot of tea, please? I need to put my feet up. All this flying around seems to have caught up to me."

Tom, who had been reading the newspaper he had purchased at the airport, jumped up and said, "Oh, Rose, I'm so sorry. Look, sit down and I'll make us both a bite to eat. Here, read the paper while I make the tea."

Rose smiled. That was the old Tom. He had been a bit strained since picking her up. *He must have something on his mind,* she thought as she sat down. Suddenly, though, Rose jumped up again.

"Oh, Tom, I completely forgot. I must phone Susan Parker and tell her about Cynthia Mc Ardle." With that she grabbed the phone and dialled Susan's cell phone number. It was answered almost immediately.

"Inspector Susan Parker speaking. How may I help you?"

SERGEANT FLOWERS and Constable Mathieson pulled up beside the bright, red Honda Civic sitting in the snow-covered driveway. It was obvious that no one had left the house for a while as the snow lay undisturbed all the way up the driveway to the front door.

The two officers knocked first and then taking a run, they both rammed the front door. Nothing happened and they both laughed after rubbing their rather bruised shoulders. "They make it look pretty easy in the movies." Constable Mathieson said, "Why don't we just break one of the bedroom windows and climb in that way?"

They chose the smallest of the side windows and soon Constable Mathieson had squeezed his body through and climbed inside. Five minutes later he opened the front door looking ashen faced and visibly shocked.

"YOU HAD BETTER COME QUICKLY. Prepare yourself. It's not a pretty sight." With that the Constable shot forward and vomited into the snow-covered hedgerow at the side of the house.

Gillian lay in a pool of thick, dark, treacly blood. She was found in her study. Her head had been smashed in, presumably from behind. It looked as if she had been sitting at her computer when the perpetrator had entered and bashed her over the head.

She was dressed in a pair of black, silky pyjamas and even in death her toned body looked spectacular.

For the second time in a space of one hour, Inspector Parker received a phone call that would drastically alter the state of the inquiry.

SEVEN

Rose got up feeling refreshed and ready to face the week ahead. The upcoming weekend was Family Day and The Town Hall's big fundraiser, Soups On. Rose had volunteered to make soup for the Town Hall. There was a bit of a competition to see who would win the best soup. For three years running the best soup award had gone to one of the local restaurants. This year the committee had decided to put restaurants into a separate category. Rose had not decided yet which soup to make. She looked at her watch. It was only eight o'clock. She could go to the fitness class at the community centre and then start her cooking afterwards. The telephone rang. It was Jessica.

"Hi, Mom. Just checking to see that everything is still on for March break. Oh, and we thought that, if it's alright with you, we would like to come down for Family Day. Is that okay?"

. . .

"WELL, yes, darling, but I will be at the Town Hall serving up soup so if you don't mind that then we would love to see you."

"Of course, it's all weather permitting," Jessica said. She sounded a bit distracted.

"Is everything, alright, love?" Rose said, praying that it was.

"Oh, yes, Mom, it's just this winter. It's just got me down. But I know what I wanted to ask you. It was on CTV last night. You know that man, Jim Reynolds, the man who was involved with your old school friend, Susan? Well, he is apparently on the run here in Canada. I would watch out if I were you. Weren't you responsible for discovering that whole scam? Anyway, just be warned. Keep your eyes and ears open."

Rose took a deep breath. She could not believe that Jim Reynolds would have the nerve to return to Canada. Last she had heard he was on the run somewhere in Turkey, having left Austria shortly after Tom and she had reported seeing him in Vienna. That incident still made Rose cringe.

They should have reported seeing him in the café right away instead of waiting until they got back to the hotel and only then contacting Susan.

If they had acted more quickly, Jim would probably have been apprehended and would not still be on the loose today.

She put the phone down and called to Tom. There was no answer. Rose walked into their bedroom only to find Tom fast asleep with Ben and Puff lying sprawled out on the bed beside him.

She tiptoed out of the room and went back into the kitchen. *I'll make Tom's favourite lemon and cranberry scones*, she thought, *and I'll forgo my fitness class too*. It was time that Tom and she spent some quality time with just each other.

THE WHOLE DAY had been spent at Gillian Jeffries house working alongside the Crime Scene Investigators. Everyone who entered had to wear white, disposable coveralls, white booties, and latex gloves.

Forensics spent hours dusting for fingerprints, taking swabs of this and that and bagging up all number of items from Gillian's computer from old photograph albums to scrap books, even the contents of her fridge were taken away for examination.

It was at the crime scene that Susan bumped into Peter Joyce again. He was taking photographs of the body in the study when Susan walked in.

"Ah, Inspector Parker, we meet again. We'll have to stop meeting like this." Peter laughed and put his camera down to look at her with his steady and direct gaze. He continued to chat amicably.

"It is incomprehensible to me that there should be two murders within a space of one week in such a tiny village. I would like to bet that the two are connected somehow, don't you think?"

Susan retorted rather hastily, "I'm not paid to speculate, Mr. Joyce. We deal in facts, and right now the brutal fact is that we have a murdered woman on our hands, and I need to collect evidence so that we can build a case. If you could get me the photographs as soon as possible it would be much appreciated."

Peter looked suitably taken aback by her tone. He must have misread the signs. The other day he had felt only warmth and, indeed, some chemistry between them. Today she was all cold and business like. Fickle was the word that came to his mind.

SUSAN, by the end of the day, felt thoroughly exhausted. She was too tired even for a swim. By nine o'clock she had taken herself off to bed, and even though she tried, sleep eluded her.

Finally, she had slept so badly that in the end she decided to stop fighting her insomnia and just get up. Once up, she thought, well, what now? She decided that the only place in the village that could possibly be open at two in the morning might be the supermarket.

When it first opened the previous summer there had been a lot of publicity over the fact that it was to be open twenty-four hours a day, but Susan wasn't sure if that still applied in the middle of winter. Whatever, she had to get out of her room to escape the thoughts of Jim which had crippled her ability to sleep. Why could she simply not hate the man?

They had been good together and, as with Henri, the chemistry between them had been phenomenal. But Jim had been married, and they were carrying on an illicit affair whichever way she tried to convince herself otherwise. No. Jim Reynolds was bad news, and she should just shake all feelings for him off like a wet dog.

Susan grabbed her thick, woollen jacket and pulled on her fleece lined winter boots. She pulled down a knitted toque onto her head and left the room quietly. There had been no fresh snow that night, but it was bitingly cold. *I must be mad going out into the freezing Arctic air,* she thought as she reversed her car and pulled away from The Bayfield Village Inn.

Driving down the highway seemed strange and lonely

being the single, solitary vehicle on the road with all the lights out throughout the village. Susan decided to drive up Short Hill to Bayfield Terrace. She wanted to just drive past Rose and Tom's house. If Jim was in the area Rose could possibly be a target if he was seeking retribution.

I am being an alarmist, Susan thought as she slowed down in front of the Blair house and looked around. All was as it should be. She continued to drive around until she came to Glass Street. Susan could see in the distance the yellow police tape surrounding the house fluttering in the breeze.

The gruesome murder of Gillian Jeffries still lingered large in her mind. Whoever had killed the poor woman had shown considerable anger. Her head had been hammered so hard that the skull had been reduced to a bloody pulp.

Susan shuddered at the thought and drove on back to Blair Street, onto Jane, and continued to the highway. Arriving at the supermarket, she found that it was indeed closed. She drove back to her motel slowly suddenly feeling incredibly tired and very lonely.

SUSAN ENTERED HER BEDROOM, stripped off her clothing, and jumped back into her warm bed. Her eyes shut fast and within minutes she was engulfed in a deep sleep.

EIGHT

Susan was woken up by the shrill sound of her cell phone ringing. She looked at the clock and fairly jumped out of bed. It was eight-thirty.

She was already thirty minutes late for her staff briefing. Susan snatched up the phone knowing full well who the caller would be. Sure enough it was Sergeant Flowers wondering if everything was alright.

Susan assured him that she had been delayed but would be at The Lion's Hall shortly. She grabbed her clothes, ran to the bathroom, and quickly washed her face and brushed her teeth.

No time for either a shower or a swim, Susan thought as she brushed her hair and quickly applied some lipstick. Within ten minutes of the Sergeant's call, she was at The Lion's Hall.

She was about to enter the room when she was halted by the sound of Sergeant Flowers voice acting out her role as team leader. She had to admit that he sounded suitably authoritative and impressive, but was he taking the micky out of her or was he seriously taking the initiative? She continued to listen as he talked.

"Team, we need to seriously analyse all of the events leading up to the murder of Joe Berry and try to establish some logical timeline. Then we need to find the three main-stays of all inquiries: means, motive, and opportunity.

We all know the means, the kitchen knife, but who even knew where the knives were kept in the kitchen? Only the town hall committee members knew the brand-new knife that Rose Blair had bought was still in its packaging in the kitchen.

As to opportunity, this is where we have to go back and analyse the information that we actually have at hand and create a logical timeline. When it comes to motive, we need to re-examine what we have discovered from our friend Cynthia and try and find out where Gillian Jeffries fits into all of this. Now..."

Susan stepped into the room interrupting the Sergeant, saying briskly, "Thank you, Sergeant. We will get back to this in a minute but right now we need to address the murder of Gillian Jeffries.

As you know, the Crime Squad was at the Jeffries house for six hours yesterday. They took away her computer and hopefully will get back to me within twenty-four hours to let us know the contents.

Right, now in ninety percent of murders of this nature the prime suspect turns out to be the nearest and dearest to the victim. In this case that would be the ex-husband, Andy Jeffries. They had been married thirty-one years before the divorce. That's a long time for anyone.

We need to question Mr. Jeffries as soon as possible. In fact, I need to go back to London for a face-to-face meeting with the 'boss' so I will arrange for him to be brought in for questioning while I'm there.

In the meantime, Sergeant, I would like you to conduct a thorough background search on Andy Jeffries. Leave no stone unturned."

Susan looked at her watch. As soon as the briefing was over, she would call up Headquarters and get the ball moving on the Jeffries case, but right now she would continue with the line of enquiry her Sergeant had been pursuing when she had first arrived.

She got hold of a dry erase marker and wrote on the white board 'Time, 6:00' and next to the time she wrote, 'Arrivals, Peggy G.' On the one side of the board, she wrote the time and continued to scribe while her team helped to fill in the details. The chart looked like this:

TIME	ARRIVALS
6:00	Peggy G.
6:00	Cynthia
7:15	Rose and Tom
7:25	The Berries
7:30	Gillian J.
7:40	Joe and Gillian

So, we know that Tom Blair overheard Gillian and Joe arguing at around 7:40. Do we have any times for when the various band members or Cynthia left the room?"

Constable Brown pulled out his iPad and slid his fingers across the screen until he got to his list of notes. "Ma'am, I have here that Cynthia went to the washroom just before heading upstairs to perform. Time was approximately 7:50.

She claims to have been in the wings for a good five minutes before her performance started."

Susan wrote 7:50 on the chart with Cynthia's name next to it. "Any other times to add?" She said while all the team flicked through their notes or social devices. Half of the team were into technology while the other half, notably the older ones, still used the traditional handwritten notebooks.

Constable Mathieson said, "Well, I have written down here that Bill Branson stepped out for a quick smoke at 8:15 but he is adamant that Joe Berry was still alive then as he saw him talking to Adam."

Susan wrote on her chart: 8:15 Bill B. (outside)

"What time was Joe Berry actually found?"

Sergeant Flowers consulted his notebook. "According to my notes we received a phone call from Rose Blair at 8:40. Peggy Griersen had just discovered the body."

Susan wrote on the white board: 8:35? Joe Berry dead – and 8:40 Rose Blair phone call. She stood back to look at the now quite detailed timeline.

"Good work. Now we have a timeline which will hopefully help us with the opportunity side of the equation. Let's move on though, as I have some interesting information which hopefully might move this case along.

Rose Blair just returned from Nova Scotia where she was visiting her daughter. Anyhow, she found out some very revealing facts about Cynthia McArdle. Cynthia and Joe Berry were an 'item' until she found herself pregnant. This all took place in her first year at university. She stalked Joe to the point that he had to take out a restraining order on her.

Now, what I want to know is why did she deny all knowledge of knowing Joe? Constable Mathieson, any further on interviewing Cynthia?"

"Yes ma'am. I contacted the Dartmouth Police, and they

were going to bring her in for questioning. They will phone when she is in the interviewing room and will hook us up to a secure video link."

"Thank you, Constable. Now, I did go and talk to Bill Jenson and from our conversation it is clear that, although he no longer held a grudge towards our victim, he still did not particularly like the man. I do not think that he is our murderer. He doesn't have a very strong motive for murder.

No, Cynthia is still our prime suspect although I still don't think that she could have actually murdered Joe. According to Tom Blair, he dropped her off at her aunts in Clinton the day before Gillian Jeffries was murdered.

And what about Gillian Jeffries? It appears that Tom might have been the last person to have seen her alive. That was on Sunday night.

We think, but this will have to be confirmed by forensics, that Gillian was murdered later on that night. So, you see, we either have two murderers in our midst or else Cynthia is not our prime suspect.

Now, on a completely different note, I need to bring to your attention the fact that Jim Reynolds is more than likely coming back to this area. For those of you unfamiliar with the case history, Jim Reynolds is wanted on three counts of murder.

He eluded us two years ago by escaping to Europe where he was spotted by Interpol several times, most recently in Istanbul. He is a dangerous man. His family live in Wingham, but he may also want to settle a few scores here in Bayfield. Tom and Rose Blair were largely responsible for breaking open the case, and it is because of them that we were able to uncover the huge scam setup which was masterminded by Jim himself. I am concerned for the Blairs' safety. From now on I want you all to take it in turns to be on the surveillance team, but I don't want to alarm Tom and Rose so be discreet. Right, I'll draw up a rota and pin it up on the board here.

Sergeant, any idea when the interview with Cynthia McArdle will take place?"

"Umm…, no, ma'am. They will let us know as soon as they've brought her in for questioning."

Susan drummed her fingers on the table impatiently. She raised her voice to almost a shout of pure exasperation. "It's always such a waiting game. I could have flown to Halifax myself and interviewed the blasted woman by now. Why is it taking them so long?"

Sergeant Flowers looked down at his feet and kept his silence.

"I'm sorry. I shouldn't take it out on you. It's just that this whole case hinges on interviewing Cynthia McArdle. We've got a double murder on our hands so you would think that would be enough to fire the Dartmouth Police into action! Well team, we'll take a break for the day. Be back again tomorrow and hopefully we might have our prime suspect interviewed by then. I'm going to talk to Rose Blair again and see if there is anything else she can remember from the Dart-mouth shopkeeper."

While the rest of the team packed up their papers and prepared to leave for the day, Susan picked up her cell phone and called the London Forensics Department. After a short conversation she slammed her hands on the table and shouted,

"Give me a break. We need to know the time of death and now!"

Next, she put in a call to the Crime Squad and requested that a Mr. Andrew Jeffries be brought in for questioning that afternoon. Susan then confirmed her meeting which had been set for 2:00 p.m. The last call she made was to Rose. She wanted to let her know about Gillian Jeffries murder.

With that done she closed her phone and packed up her laptop. Susan hastily left the Lion's Building. It was snowing great, big, white flakes and her car was almost buried. Susan reached for her snow scraper and began to clear off the ice. It would take her a good hour and a half to get to the Headquarters building on Richmond, in London. If she was to set off now, she could grab a bite to eat in Exeter or Lucan and still be on time for her meeting at two.

ROSE LOOKED out of the window and let out a deep sigh. It certainly was a winter wonderland with the trees and shrubs all shrouded in white. She longed however to see greenery again.

Maybe she and Tom should join the majority of villagers who flew south each year, like the snowbirds who escaped the winter. Bayfield was like a ghost town down the main street with ninety percent of the shops closed and only a few restaurants open. Rose sighed again. If truth be known she felt a bit lonely.

Since the death of her good friend, Mary Stokes, a big, empty hole had been left in Rose's heart.

There were other friends, but no one as close as she had been with Mary. They had been like sisters together and now that she was gone there had been no one else to replace that closeness.

Tom came up behind Rose and wrapped his arms around her, "Penny for your thoughts, love?" He said as he kissed the back of her neck.

"Oh, Tom, I was just thinking about Mary and how much I miss her. I'm feeling a bit low in spirits today."

"Never mind, love. Look it's quite beautiful outside. Why don't we wrap up and take the dogs for a walk? A bit of fresh air will do you a world of good."

They were just putting on their winter boots when the telephone rang. Rose answered.

"Oh, hi, Susan." Rose listened and then let out a little cry. "Oh my gosh, Susan, that's dreadful, absolutely awful." They spoke a little longer and then Rose said, "Of course, come around tomorrow. Why don't you come for dinner? We've got nothing much planned for today or tomorrow. Yes, I'm still feeling a bit tired after my trip back from Halifax. Okay. What about six o'clock? Great. See you then."

Rose put the phone down and turned to Tom.

"Gillian Jeffries has been found dead. Murdered. Oh, Tom, this all feels like déjà vu. I can't go through another murder. It's bad enough that Joe Berry was killed but he wasn't a resident of Bayfield."

Tom pulled Rose to him and kissed her. His own mind was racing. Was he the last person to have seen Gillian alive? *Oh my gosh,* he thought, *could I even be considered a murder suspect?*

THE DRIVE to London was uneventful. The roads were clear, and the sun was actually shining. Susan stopped off in Lucan and ate her lunch at The Stuffed Zucchini, located next to the Donnelly Museum. The restaurant was almost full, and Susan just managed to get the last table by the window.

THE STUFFED ZUCCHINI was essentially a Thai restaurant, but they also served a variety of standard menu items.

Susan chose their special, Pad Thai, and sat back with a cup of coffee to wait for the meal. While she was waiting, she had a text message from Officer Dryden from London Headquarters, to say that Andrew Jeffries had been brought in.

He was currently in Interview Room 5 waiting to be questioned. Susan sent a reply back telling the officer to keep him there until she arrived, and she would conduct the interview herself. She then sent another text message to Superintendent Watson asking if their meeting could be deferred to later on that day. His terse reply back was that he was busy for the rest of the afternoon. She would have to reschedule their meeting for another day.

Susan sighed. Mind you it probably was a blessing in disguise that her meeting had been cancelled as she had precious little to report, and she knew how much her boss wanted quick results. Investigations cost money and his job was to keep everything on budget.

Her Pad Thai was served and was absolutely delicious. There was nothing like a good meal to calm the nerves, Susan thought as she got out her wallet to pay. As she reached in to pull out a $20 note, Peter Joyce's business card fell out on to the counter.

Susan picked it up and made up her mind. After her interview with Andrew Jeffries, she would call Peter to apologise to him for her officious behaviour. She still didn't know why she had reacted so sharply to him the other day. He had been perfectly pleasant, and she had pretty well bitten his head off. *I'm just feeling too stressed out,* she rationalized as she pulled away in her car and set off on the last leg of her journey to London.

. . .

TWENTY MINUTES later she pulled up outside the Serious Crimes Headquarters and parked her car in the last available space in front of the building. After sleepy Bayfield, London seemed positively buzzing with people. The best compromise, Susan thought, would be to live in a city throughout the winter months and move to Bayfield in the summer. The alternative, of course, would be to head for the sun and become a snowbird.

She walked into the building and took the elevator up to the seventh floor. The Crime Squad was always crazy busy with people coming and going and long line ups of people waiting for friends, loved ones, or acquaintances to be released from the clutches of police custody.

Susan signed in, showed her warrant card to the Detaining Officer, and walked towards the interview rooms. All the rooms had a window made up of one-way viewing glass. The police could observe from the outside without being seen from the inside. Susan stood outside the observation window of Interview Room 5.

Inside, a dark-haired man sat looking extremely irritated. He was a good-looking man in a distinctly European way. He had thick, black hair and the beginnings of a black shadow around his jaw line. He wore an expensive looking charcoal grey wool jacket, a light blue Ralph Lauren linen shirt, and what looked like crisp, black pants.

Neatly folded on the adjacent chair was a dark, woollen overcoat, a grey silk scarf, and black leather gloves. The man reeked of money. Susan was a great believer in understanding body language. You could tell so much about a person through their body gestures and general demeanour.

Andrew Jeffries was not only mightily pissed off, he was a man with a great load to bare on his shoulders judging by how high they were up by his ears. He did not look a happy man. He might be wealthy, but, in Susan's experience, rarely was wealth synonymous with happiness. She knocked on the door and entered.

"Good afternoon Mr. Jeffries. My name is Inspector Parker. I'm here to question you in relation to your ex-wife's murder." Susan extended her hand to the man who stood up and shook her hand graciously. They both sat down.

"I do have to caution you that anything you say will be recorded and could be used in court. If you want to have a lawyer present you must notify me straight away before I continue this interview."

Andy nodded and spoke for the first time. He had a quiet but commanding voice and an engaging manner.

"No, I have nothing to hide, but I do have a business to run and would appreciate it if we could get this over with as soon as possible. I have already been here for over an hour."

Susan couldn't blame the man. She, too, would be feeling mightily cheesed off if she had been kept waiting for so long.

"Right. Let's get on with it then." She said briskly at the same time pressing the record button and nodding to the attending officer.

"What is your full name?"

"Andrew Lloyd Jeffries."

"Age"

"I was born on April 27, 1963, in Peterborough."

Susan smiled. He had pre-empted her next question.

"Okay, now moving on. Could you tell me about your relationship with the deceased? Where and when did you first meet Gillian Jeffries?"

"We met and got married in 1982 in Peterborough. We are both from that area."

Susan suddenly saw a cloud pass over Andy's eyes. He

had realized that he was talking about his wife as if she was still alive.

"Oh, I see why you've dragged me in for questioning. You think that I killed my ex-wife?"

Bingo, thought Susan, but she smiled gently and resumed her questioning without blinking an eye.

"Mr. Jeffries, why did you and Gillian divorce?"

Andy paused a minute and then spoke with a bitter tongue.

"She was having an affair with my partner and I found out."

"YOUR PARTNER? By that I assume you mean your business partner?"

"Yes. We set up Howell and Jeffries Chartered Accountants ten years ago. Brad Howell and I have built up this company by sheer hard work alone.

When I discovered that Gillian and Brad had been sleeping together for three years, well, I went ballistic and threw her out."

"What about your partner? Did you throw him out too?" Susan asked with a glint in her eyes.

"No. We are business partners, but we moved offices. I am on one floor of the building now and he is on the other. We don't speak to each other. Only through joint business matters do we communicate."

"That's a sad state of affairs. What about Mr. Howell's family? Does he have a wife?"

Once again Andy went quiet.

"Inspector Parker, do you have any idea what kind of impact a divorce has on all concerned? Brad's wife and children left him. They had a house off Windermere Road which backed on to the river. Amy and the kids ended up moving back to Whitby where her family is from. Gillian and I never had children, but we had to sell our lovely home in Byron, and now I live in a small condo here, downtown. All our lives had been turned upside down by Gillian and Brad's indiscretion."

The pain and bitterness were palpable. Susan could remember what it felt like going through a divorce, although, with her there had been no children involved and she had only been married a few short years.

Her husband had been a philandering jerk and she was well rid of him. But still, her family had been suitably shocked and yes, it did have repercussions, the biggest one being Susan's career change.

As she got older, she realized that in the big picture everything had a reason. In her case, her divorce, and subsequent leaving of her first career, teaching, had both been a blessing in disguise. She had never been happy in her role as teacher.

The Catholic school she had taught at had frowned upon her for getting a divorce and that had made her resign in a fit of peeve. How could they have been so judgemental in those days? The subsequent struggle to change her life had not been easy.

Going through the police academy all those years ago, when there were only a handful of women entering the force, had been tough. But in retrospect, Susan wouldn't have changed anything, other than maybe the two mistakes that she had made, one by marrying the jerk, and two by entering the wrong profession in the first place.

"I understand your bitterness. Now, can I ask you to account for your movements from Sunday through to Wednesday of this week?"

Andy answered quickly. "I was where I always am, either

in my office or in my condo here in London."

"MR. JEFFRIES, could you be more specific on the timing of your movements during the evening of last Sunday? Were you in your office or your condo, and do you have any witnesses as to where you were that evening?"

Susan was beginning to get a little irritated by the man's flippancy.

Andy chewed his lip and replied quietly, "I was actually in my office most of the day on Sunday. I didn't leave until around 7:30 p.m. as I was working on a file that I needed to have finished by Monday. Thinking about it, I do have a witness to that. Security does a walk through the building several times over the weekend, and I talked to the security guard on duty that evening just before I left. I believe it was at around 7:00 p.m. I can provide you with the name and contact numbers for the agency that supplies the security staff.

As to later that evening, well, I'm afraid I went home; cooked myself some eggs and bacon, opened a beer, and sat in front of the television where I promptly fell asleep. Something I do a lot these days."

Susan did a quick calculation. If what he said could be corroborated then it was still possible for him to have jumped into his car, driven to Bayfield, confronted Gillian, and still be back in London before midnight. But, of course, they had no proof either way. The man could very possibly be telling the truth.

"What car do you drive?"

"I drive a Toyota Avalon."

"What colour?"

"Silver. It's a 2012 model saloon."

"Okay. You do know that we will be able to verify your story one way or another, so it is in your best interest to be telling the truth?"

Andy fidgeted in his seat and looked down at the floor.

"Yes, I know that, but I did not murder Gillian. Granted there were times when I really felt that I could have but I did not. When I was notified of her murder, my first reaction was one of complete shock. It surprised me how very sad I felt at the news. Although she was unfaithful to me, we did have good times together. She was a very fun loving and beautiful woman."

"Tell me about her business venture Time for Toning. How did she finance this?"

"Part of the divorce settlement went into paying for the building. She was always quite shrewd. She not only got the business up and running, but it was beginning to make her good money. I believe she had a strong membership base. I actually was very impressed by her business acumen."

"Did you help her with the bookkeeping side of things being an accountant yourself?"

"No way. I don't think that you understand, when Gillian and I divorced neither of us wanted anything to do with each other. Gillian set up her business entirely on her own. The reason why I know so much about it is not through Gillian, but my friend Ron who is her accountant.

He obviously never talks specifics, but he has told me how well she was doing. I do confess to feeling a level of pride in her ability to start and run a thriving business all by herself."

"Now, Mr. Jeffries, we were told that your wife knew Joe Berry, the man who was murdered at the Town Hall last Saturday night. Can you give us any information about this relationship?"

Andy looked pensive. Susan could see that he had been taken by surprise with her turn in questioning. Finally, he answered. "Gillian, many years ago before we met, had her own band called Gillian and the Jangles. She would have been in her early twenties at the time. I believe that she met The Berries at one of their gigs. She told me that she'd had a fling with Joe Berry. As far as I can recall that is all it was, just a brief relationship back when she was a single girl and, in the groove, so to speak."

"So, as far as you know, she was not in any contact with Joe Berry since then?"

"No, not as far as I know, but who knows with Gillian. She was her own person in every way, and maybe she was still meeting up with him. If that was the case, I never knew about it. But, hey, I'm the sucker who didn't know that she was having an affair with my partner, and that was happening right under my nose!"

Susan could see that she wouldn't get much more out of him. She thanked him for coming in and showed him to the door, saying, "We will be in touch, Mr. Jeffries."

After the interview, Susan decided that she had time to pop back to her house in Wortley Village and check on it before visiting with Peter Joyce. Susan had bought a lovely Ontario cottage on Edward Street and had spent many months renovating it to the way she wanted.

Entering the front door, she looked around at the cosy living room. There was a stone fireplace in which she had installed a very realistic gas insert. This she ignited and instantly the room took on a comforting warm glow. Susan left the heating on low to keep the pipes from freezing. It wasn't worth cranking up the heat, as she couldn't stay more than an hour or so. The little fireplace, however, had a fan which instantly blew out a fair amount of heat.

· · ·

SUSAN CUDDLED up on the sofa and opened her brief-case. She pulled out a file containing all the reports of the case up to date. Susan spent the following hour chasing up the forensic report and reading through all the investigation notes. Were they missing something? She reread all the band members statements again. Bill Jenson had been interviewed quite rigorously but the other two band members, the drummer, John Selbrook, and the lead guitarist, Adam Frank, both had rather sketchy statements. *Maybe these men should be interviewed again,* Susan thought as she flicked through all the statements the officers had collected.

Interviewing Cynthia McArdle hopefully would reveal much more information. Susan telephoned the Halifax Police division. The phone was picked up right away.

"This is Inspector Susan Parker, Homicide division, London Branch of Serious Crimes. I need to know why Cynthia McArdle has not yet been brought in for questioning regarding a double murder?"

There was a pause on the other end of the line and then a deep, gruff voice said,

"She is in our interview room right now. I was about to contact you, but you beat me to it. Do you want us to question her first or do you want a first go at her?"

Susan thought quickly and answered, "Well, if you could establish the basics, date of birth, family background, etc., then set up a video conference call so that I can link up with you through my computer that would be great."

Susan put her phone down and pulled out her laptop. "We might finally get some answers from Ms. McArdle," she muttered as she waited for the secure connection.

Ten minutes later she had the very angry looking face of Cynthia McArdle snarling at her from her computer screen. "Good afternoon, Ms. McArdle. You probably remember me from a week ago in Bayfield. I came around to Rose and Tom Blair's house where you were billeted. My name is Inspector Parker and I have a few questions to ask you. According to my notes, you flatly denied ever knowing Joe Berry. I quote, 'I have to confess to not being a particular fan of The Berries.' They were popular way before my time. How old actually are you?"

Cynthia looked like she was about to say something when she stopped herself. She had already given her date of birth to the local officer who had first interviewed her. She mumbled, "I'm sixty-four." Susan nodded and then went on to the next question.

"Did you ever have a relationship with Joe Berry?"

Cynthia answered too quickly, "No, of course not. I barely knew the man."

"Oh, come on, Cynthia, stop denying the fact that you were madly in love with Joe Berry when you were a student. I have already established that you were his girlfriend in your first year at McGill University, and that after he split with you, Joe had to take out a restraining order as you were stalking him everywhere. Is it not also true that you got pregnant and that Joe was the father? What happened to the baby and did Joe even know that he was a father?"

Cynthia had gone quite pale, and her eyes seemed to visibly bulge. She started to stammer and just for a moment Susan felt a bit sorry for her.

"How dare you bring all of that up? It is all in the past and I don't ever want to be reminded of my misspent youth. Yes, I dated Joe Berry for a year. I thought that he loved me and no, I didn't stalk him. I just couldn't get used to not being part of his life anymore. Oh, and Joe never knew that I was pregnant. I had the baby and gave it up for adoption right away."

"You're saying Joe never even knew that he had a child by you? Was it a girl or a boy?"

"No. I never told him. If you must know, I gave birth to a beautiful baby boy. I only held him once before they took him away. I don't know what any of this has to do with the death of Joe Berry."

"Did Joe know who you were when you arrived at the Town Hall in Bayfield?"

"Well, he must have as I haven't changed my name. He barely glanced my way when we were in the meeting room of the Town Hall. My agent got me the gig so he may not have known that I had actually been booked. I swear that he was far too preoccupied with that slut, what's her name, Gillian Jeffries, the fitness instructor. I heard them arguing, you know. They were going at it like hammer and tongs. I then had to go upstairs to perform, so I never heard the outcome, but if you ask me, I'd put my money on her as being the murderer."

"So, what about the other band members? The drummer and the lead guitarist? Did they leave the room at all or have any arguments with Joe?"

"Look, Inspector, I've already gone over this with you. The two guitarists seemed rather preoccupied with tuning their guitars and the drummer just sat in the corner of the room with his eyes closed.

The only person who left the room, as far as I can remember, was Joe and, as I've already told you, he could be heard arguing with that woman. Now, that really is all I can tell you."

"Well, Ms. McArdle, that woman as you put it, was found murdered yesterday . Did you know her at all?"

Cynthia's face turned a scarlet red. She shouted back at the screen with a face contorted with anger. "No, I did not know the bitch. Look, I made the mistake of falling in love with Joe Berry when I was just nineteen. That's over forty years ago, and no, I did not murder Joe nor that woman. Now can I please leave? I am rapidly losing my patience with your covert and overt questions."

Susan stared coldly at Cynthia.

"Did you not have a restraining order slapped upon you for stalking Joe Berry?"

"Oh, give me a break. As I said, that was over forty years ago. I was young and gullible and had never experienced unrequited love."

"If you were stalking Joe, then you might just remember him dating Gillian Jeffries. She was the lead singer in the band called Gillian and the Jangles. I believe that they dated for a year or so right about the time that Joe took out a restraining order on you."

Cynthia glowered and shouted out. "I told you, I was young and silly. Maybe I can remember Joe dating a singer, but I didn't know her name was Gillian. She was just a common slut anyway."

"But you had Joe's baby, so what does that make you? Why did you never tell Joe that he had a son?"

Cynthia's face crumpled. She quietly muttered, "I wanted him to love me and not the baby." She began to sob openly.

Susan concluded the interview and thanked the Dartmouth officer before clicking off the computer. Sitting back on the sofa she slowly revisited the whole interview again in her head. The inquiry was finally getting somewhere.

. . .

IT WAS six o'clock in the evening before Susan drove into Peter Joyce's driveway. She had telephoned him beforehand and he had sounded very surprised to hear her voice.

"Sure, come on over. I've just got my dinner ready. If you don't mind eating chili, please feel free to join me."

Susan stopped off at the local LCBO and bought a bottle of wine. She arrived at his door and looked around. His house was a split ranch style, well maintained and tidy in the front. His battered Jeep sat in the driveway. Peter came to the door wearing casual blue jeans and a blue sweatshirt. His hair looked as if it was still wet and was combed back off his face revealing and accentuating the startling blue of his eyes. He was a handsome man, Susan thought.

"COME ON IN. Welcome to my humble abode."

Susan entered and the minute she came inside her breath was taken away by the photographs displayed on every possible piece of wall space. They all looked fantastic. Some were in black and white and others in full colour.

"Wow, these are all wonderful. I'm assuming that this is all your own work?"

Peter smiled and nodded.

"Some of these go back many years. In fact, I can plot my whole career by them. This collection," he pointed to three photographs with massive mountains in the background and huge eagles or what looked like eagles, sitting in nests in the foreground, "I shot twenty years ago on my first overseas shoot with National Geographic. They are Nepalese Condor's. I had to be taken up in a light aircraft and then hung out the window to get these shots."

"Now these," he pointed to a collection of smaller prints, which Susan recognized immediately "were my first ever professional photographs that I took in Montreal way back in 1976. I grew up there, you know."

Susan looked at the man. He was so talented and had led such an interesting life. Montreal in the seventies, that rang a bell.

"Did you ever go to one of The Berries concerts? They were big in the seventies in Montreal?"

"Actually, I did. They were very popular, and I got to cover the photographs for Life magazine with The Berries as the main story. Talking of Montreal, there is something I meant to tell you. That gal, Gillian something, you know, the poor woman who was murdered in Bayfield, I saw her playing in Montreal too. It must have been that same year I was on the staff of Life Magazine and my job was to cover the pop scene. Well, there was this group called Gillian and the Jangles, an all women band with Gillian as the lead singer. Women bands were quite rare in those days and they were quite good. Anyway, I dug these photographs out to show you. Here you are."

SUSAN LOOKED at a black and white photograph of four young women all wearing their hair long. They had scarves tied around their heads and long beads around their necks. Susan could tell right away which one was Gillian Jeffries. She stood out as the most attractive of the women by far. She had a sultry, sexy look about her, and a fantastic figure emphasised by a black cat suit, skintight and totally revealing of all her curves. Gillian looked like a girl in control of her life in every way.

The other photographs showed all four girls in action. Two played the guitar and one, the drums. Gillian obviously was the singer in the band. They looked happy and carefree and quite professional.

"These are great, Peter. Can I keep them? I'll get them back to you when the investigation is over. Would that be okay?"

"Sure. I would like them back, though, as I like to keep a record of all my work. Now, dinner is ready. Can I get you a glass of wine?"

The next couple of hours passed by wonderfully. By the end of the evening Susan felt as if she had known Peter all her life, although, as she drove home to her cottage in Wortley where she had decided to spend the night, she realized just how little she had actually found out about Peter's personal life. For instance, had he been married? Was he divorced? Maybe he preferred men? Did he have any children? So many unanswered questions flashed through her mind.

Mind you, Susan thought, she hadn't exactly talked about her own personal life either. Peter had glanced at her ring, but he had not made any comment. At the end of the evening Susan had thanked him for the lovely meal and they had promised to get in touch sometime.

Lying in bed in the cosy bedroom of her Ontario cottage, Susan replayed the evening in her mind. She felt very attracted to Peter Joyce, yet knew she was playing with fire. Firstly, she had only just met the man and more importantly, she was engaged to Henri. She did not want to complicate her life further, particularly as she and Henri had pretty well decided that they would get married in the summer and that he would retire and move to London.

But still, Peter Joyce intrigued her, of that she was sure.

NINE

Susan arrived back in Bayfield just in time for the morning briefing. The drive from London had been slow as the roads were treacherously icy. Susan had passed three cars in the ditch and had witnessed one nasty accident. Generally, people drove sensibly in winter conditions, but there were always a few silly people who drove far too fast on the icy roads and then ended up causing an accident.

The team was gathered, and the smell of coffee wafted through the door as Susan entered the building.

"Good morning everyone," Susan greeted her team cheerfully. At least she had something positive to report, indeed, two positive reports if she counted her interview with Cynthia McArdle as well as that of Andrew Jeffries. She proceeded to outline what she had learnt from her interview with Andrew Jeffries, concluding with a crisp, "Has anyone any questions?"

The room went quiet. Susan continued.

"I finally got to interview Cynthia McArdle. She was besotted with Joe Berry when they were first year students at McGill. Unfortunately, it was unrequited love and they split up. Cynthia was already pregnant with Joe's child. He never knew about the baby. She gave birth to a baby boy who was then put up for adoption."

Sergeant Flowers interrupted Susan, "Ma'am, do we have any details of the adoption?"

Susan hated being interrupted, but the Sergeant did have a point.

"No, we don't, Sergeant, but we will when you've done your research."

Constable Elliot got up and walked over to Susan. He was carrying a large, brown envelope.

"Oh, I almost forgot, ma'am, this was couriered here this morning." The Constable put it on the table next to Susan's laptop.

Susan opened it and found a yellow sticky tab note stuck to a sheath of papers, which, when she glanced through, were the hard copies of Gillian Jeffries email account going back at least a month. Along with the email copies, there was a rather worn and tatty looking scrap book. She flicked through it and immediately stopped, saying out loud, "Good gosh."

The rest of the team, who were getting ready to leave, suddenly went silent as Susan continued to look through the scrap book, this time more slowly.

"Team, we have proof that our Gillian Jeffries knew Joe Berry pretty darn well. This is a scrap book just crammed full of newspaper cuttings and photographs of The Berries dating back to the 70s. Look at this picture." She held up the scrap book and pointed to an old black and white photo of the band. They all looked like young hippies with shoulder length hair and tight-fitting t-shirts and jeans. They did look unbelievably young, Susan thought.

"IT LOOKS like she avidly followed the groups rise to fame." Susan passed the scrap book around for everyone to peruse. She then started reading the emails. They were hugely revealing in themselves.

"Fucking hell," Susan swore, "This is bordering on pornography. Talk about sexually explicit."

Gillian had received a number of emails from Joe describing how he would like to devour various parts of her body and what he would like to do with her regarding whips, hand cuffs, and all kinds of S&M references. He declared his lust for her in a multitude of ways, but most revealing of all was that he had planned his visit to Bayfield, solely with mind to spending a few days of extremely kinky sex with Gillian.

References to "over the years," inferred that their relationship had spanned a few decades.

Susan wondered just what had caused the argument at the Town Hall, as according to the emails, they were both steamy under the collar waiting for each other. By the sounds of things, they couldn't wait to jump into bed together.

Reading through the emails made Susan blush. *Fifty Shades of Grey, eat your heart out*, Susan thought as she continued to read the very explicit emails. She had thought that Henri and she had a pretty hot thing going, but it paled in comparison to Gillian and Joe's sex life. Of course, Susan thought, much of this could be pure fantasy so she changed her line of thought to the more practical matter of how the couple actually met.

They must have been pretty discreet with their liaisons as

the other band members obviously knew nothing about what was going on. The big question was, did Cynthia McArdle know that someone was as besotted with Joe Berry as herself? Would that have been motive enough for murder? All these thoughts, and more, rushed through Susan's head as she distributed the copies of the email printouts to her team to read.

Susan's stomach grumbled. She realized that she had skipped breakfast and was now starving. Wrapping up the meeting, she looked at her watch. It was almost twelve. She had time to drive into Goderich to do some shopping and maybe get her hair done too before going around to Rose and Tom's house for dinner.

ROSE LOOKED AT HER WATCH. It was already 5:00 p.m. and she hadn't even begun to prepare their dinner. Tom had fallen asleep in front of the fire in the living room and Ben and Puff had joined their master. All three of them were gently snoring away.

Rose got out the stewing steak that she had bought from Foodland and some bacon which she had bought from the Mennonite market. She began to prepare it by cutting the steak into nice chunks roughly an inch in size. She chopped up some onion, garlic, and mushrooms, poured some olive oil into a saucepan, and proceeded to sauté the onions and garlic until they were transparent. Tossing the steak in seasoned flour Rose added it all to the pan and browned the meat.

Opening a bottle of red wine, she poured herself a glass and then poured almost half the bottle over the meat. Stirring the whole lot up, she brought it all to a boil and then turned the plate down to simmer. Then she peeled some potatoes and put those, along with some chopped kale, in a pan of water and put it on another plate to boil. She would mash the kale up with the potatoes once they were cooked and serve it with green beans and julienne carrots. But what should she make for dessert?

Rose looked over at the fruit bowl which contained apples, oranges, and three very over ripe looking bananas. She immediately knew what she would make. Peeling the bananas and slicing them lengthways, she placed them into a shallow baking dish.

Next, she sprinkled brown sugar over the fruit and poured fresh orange juice over it all, submerging the fruit in the juice. She put it in the oven to bake for thirty minutes. Rose would serve this with whipped cream.

With the meal prepared she set about laying the table. Fortunately, Rose had a small loaf of artisan bread in the freezer which she took out and placed in the microwave to thaw.

SHE WAS JUST TOSSING a salad together when Tom came ambling into the kitchen stretching his arms out over his head and yawning, "I had a little snooze, my love. Is there anything I can do?"

Rose looked at her watch again rather pointedly. "Well, Susan will be here shortly. Could you tidy up the living room and open a couple of bottles of wine. Oh, and Tom, put on some relaxing music, could you, my love?"

Norah Jones' sultry voice could be heard around the house as Rose put the finishing touches to the table. She lit a couple of red candles and placed the salad on individual side plates.

"There, it's all done with a few minutes to spare. I'm going to sit down now."

"Would you like a sherry, my love?" Tom said as he walked over towards the cocktail cabinet.

"Umm…yes, please, oh and Tom, could you put out some nuts?"

Tom poured out a sherry and opened a bottle of Guinness for himself. He was just tipping out the nuts into a couple of small bowls when the doorbell rang. It was Susan. Tom heard Rose opening the door.

"Come on in, Susan. Gosh, you look like the abominable snow man all covered in snow. I hadn't realized that it was snowing so hard."

Susan stamped her feet and great chunks of snow fell off her boots. She proceeded to unzip them. Tom came over and took her coat and hung it up in the cloak's cupboard.

Rose turned to Susan and said, "Let's go through to the sitting room. It's nice and warm in their as we've got a log fire going. What can Tom get you to drink?"

Susan thought for a minute, "Do you have a Gin and tonic? If so, I would love one."

Tom went off to get her drink while Susan followed Rose into the cosy sitting room.

"This is great. Thanks so much for inviting me over for dinner. I've begun to get tired of always eating out at restaurants. It's such a treat to be invited to eat a home cooked meal."

Tom joined the two women and soon they were feeling relaxed and chatting like old friends. Twenty minutes later Rose called them to the table for dinner. Over the boeuf-bourguignon, Susan asked Rose about Halifax, the baby, and finally she got around to talking about Cynthia McArdle.

"That was such an amazing coincidence that you were staying in Cynthia's neighbourhood. It didn't sound as if she was the most popular of women, and now that her parents have both gone, I guess that she inherited the house?"

Rose looked thoughtful, "Well, she certainly had a thing going for Joe Berry. She even stalked him after they had split up and he had to take out a restraining order on her. Mind you, she had his baby and had to give it up for adoption and that would be enough to turn anyone crazy.

According to the shopkeeper, she got involved with the drug scene after that, but she obviously managed to straighten herself out, otherwise she would never have become such an accomplished harpist. If you ask me, that Joe Berry should have been brought to account for his actions.

I almost feel sorry for what Cynthia had to go through. The trouble is that she's not the nicest of characters. She was really quite rude to Tom and me when she stayed at our house. If you ask me, she is one lady with some big issues."

"I don't think that she could have carried out the murders unless she had an accomplice as she was on stage performing at the actual time of the murder." Tom chipped in with his ever-pragmatic voice.

"Yes, well, we have ruled her out. We had Gillian Jeffries pegged as our number one prime suspect, but now that she's been murdered it appears that we are back to square one."

All three of them went quiet as they thought about Gillian Jeffries.

"Tom, you told me that you had seen Gillian the night that she was most likely murdered. What sort of mood was she in?"

Tom felt his face flush. He could hardly tell Susan about Gillian's attempted seduction.

"Umm…well, she seemed normal really."

Rose looked at Tom and could sense that he was lying.

"Why did she come around?" Susan persisted.

Tom averted his eyes and fidgeted in his seat.

"She came around to talk about the fitness club," he said lamely all the while looking bright red in the face.

Rose looked at him closely. Why was he lying so blatantly? Surely Susan could see that he was not telling her the truth. She held her breath as Susan continued to question Tom.

"Well, Tom, was she depressed or agitated or anything?"

Tom chewed on a fingernail and answered. "No, she seemed just normal."

Normal, my foot, Rose thought as she tried to change the subject. Gillian Jeffries could never have been described as normal.

"Susan, going back to Cynthia, did you check out the man who drove her to Bayfield?"

"Yes, she wanted us to leave him out of the inquiry. Apparently, he was just a one-night stand."

Rose got up and walked over to the kitchen where she opened the oven and removed the dish of flambéed bananas. Bringing it to the table she proceeded to serve out three portions.

"Mmm…that smells divine. Thank you so much for inviting me over."

They were just finishing up the dessert when Susan's phone rang. She excused herself from the table and after listening intently to the caller replied, "Yes. I'll meet you in five minutes."

She put her phone away and turned to Rose and Tom.

"So sorry, Rose, Tom, I have to leave. But once again thank you so much for the wonderful dinner."

Rose and Tom got up and walked Susan to the front door where she proceeded to put on her winter boots. Tom got out her coat and helped her into it. Susan gave Rose a quick hug and smiled at Tom.

"See you both soon." With that she rushed off into the icy night.

SERGEANT FLOWERS WAS WAITING for Susan outside The Albion. As soon as he saw her pull up, he got out of his car and walked over.

"He's inside, ma'am, over by the bar. I didn't recognize him first. He's got a thick beard and is much thinner than I remember, but it is definitely Jim Reynolds. What shall we do?"

Susan's heart had been beating at an alarming rate ever since she had got the phone call from her Sergeant. Jim Reynolds, here in Bayfield, could mean just one thing, retribution, unless he had come to see her which she doubted. Anyway, why and how would he even know that she was in Bayfield? No, he was here to settle the score, and Rose and Tom were the target.

"Sergeant, is there still a surveillance team watching the Blair's house?"

"Yes, ma'am. Constables Elliot and Brown are on duty tonight. They've reported everything quiet. Apart from your visit, there hasn't been a single car on Bayfield Terrace."

"So, how long has Jim Reynolds been at the bar?"

"I don't know exactly. I just popped in for a quick pint and then I saw him. He gave me quite a turn. I left the bar right away and came out here to phone you. I didn't want to spook him".

"You did the right thing. Now, I would like you to cover the rear exit just in case he tries to do a runner. I'm going to call Constable Mathieson and the OPP office for back up.

He's a slippery customer. If he can get past Interpol he will just as easily slip by us if we're not careful. I'm going to stay out here and wait for the back-up team."

Susan sat and thought to herself. *How can I face him and look him squarely in the eyes, this man who I felt I had known?* Her reveries were interrupted by her phone. It was a text message.

I know you are here.

Susan quickly looked up and out of her window. Snow was falling and her view of the pub was partially blocked by a man hunched up smoking a cigarette. She could just make out the window of the room where the bar was located but she could not see inside. How on earth was Jim able to see her? She got out of her car and craned her neck to get a better view. Was he watching her right now? Where was her back up team?

A black SUV pulled up in front of The Black Dog and two men got out wearing leather jackets and heavy winter boots. At first Susan did not recognize Constables Elliot and Brown. She was so used to seeing them in their uniforms. They walked over to her car.

"Reporting for duty, ma'am." Constable Elliot said while stamping his boots on the crunchy snow and clapping his hands together to get them warm. "Cold enough, eh?"

Her team looked expectantly at her. Susan thought quickly. Jim had never met either Constable Elliot or Brown. They had not been involved with the murder on Bayfield beach. It was time for some action. With Sergeant Mathieson to the rear and herself in the front, where could Jim possibly go without being seen? She would send her Constables in to arrest the man she had once loved.

"Right, men, you have both seen photographs of Jim Reynolds. According to Sergeant Mathieson, he now sports a thick, bushy beard and was last seen drinking at the bar. Approach him with caution. The man is dangerous and could possibly be armed." The men nodded and proceeded to go inside The Albion.

Susan waited anxiously outside expecting any minute to see Jim Reynolds making a run for it, but nothing happened. Soon her two Constables returned shaking their heads.

"There was no one sitting at the bar. We checked out the whole building. Only two people were drinking. The bar man said that the bearded fellow had already paid for his drinks and had left."

Susan looked to the front of the building and realized with a jolt that the cigarette smoker she had seen hunched over in the front of the building when she had first arrived must have been Jim.

"He can't have gone far. No car has left. He has to have gone on foot. You go that way," she pointed to the park, "and you can go down Main Street. I'll jump in my car. But first Constable Mathieson needs to join us." Susan picked up her phone and called the Constable's number.

"Check around the back of the building and then come around here, Sergeant. Jim is on the loose and we need to catch him before he skips the net again."

Looking down Main Street it was easy to see that there was no one around. Other than four cars parked outside The Albion and one outside The Little Inn, the street was deserted. Snow covered the road and the sidewalk. Mid-February in Bayfield looked exactly like a winter wonderland.

Susan jumped into her car and drove down Main Street, every now and then stopping to look down the sides of buildings. Her phoned chirruped. A text message had dropped in her mailbox.

You're looking good, babe.

It was Jim Reynolds.
    Susan texted back.

Where are you, Jim? You can't keep hiding.
We'll get you. Just give up now.

Jim replied.

No way Susie. I've got a few scores to settle and then it's back to Europe for me. You know, darling, you and I were so good together. I miss you, baby girl.

The text message ended abruptly. There was no point in trying to trace it. Anyway, Susan knew that he had to be very close by. But where exactly was he?

SHE DROVE right onto Catherine Street at the corner by The Little Inn and drove up to Bayfield Terrace. Even if Jim had been running, he would have been hard pushed to have got that far already.

As if in answer to her thoughts, a red Ford pick-up truck shot past her at the intersection between Colina and Catherine. It was the only other vehicle out on the road which alerted Susan. She followed it. The truck turned into Bayfield Terrace. Before Susan had time to alert her officers, to her horror, she saw the red car slow down in front of Rose and Tom's house. The next thing she heard was an almighty bang. Susan put her foot down on the accelerator as the red truck sped away down Short Hill and out onto the highway.

"Back up! Back up! Red pickup truck, license plate Charlie-Delta-Anchor 321, last seen heading north on Highway 21 out of Bayfield."

TEN

Tom was watching one of his favourite programmes on television, Law and Order. Rose was just clearing up from dinner and thinking about the ingredients for a hearty Italian Wedding soup which she had decided to make for Soups On. She had been undecided as to whether she should make her carrot and ginger soup or the Italian Wedding one, and so she had made both of them.

Ben and Puff were curled up on the sofa next to Tom. The fire was lit and the whole living room exuded a cosy charm.

"Tom, would you like a cup of tea or coffee?' Rose called out as she finished chopping the last of the vegetables.

She didn't hear his answer because suddenly the living room exploded. The front window had been blown into a million pieces.

"Tom, Tom, are you alright?" Rose shouted as she ran frantically into the living room.

Puff and Ben were barking crazily, and Tom just sat there with blood pouring down his face. Small chards of glass seemed to be embedded in his skin. He looked dazed and confused.

"MY GOSH, TOM, WHAT JUST HAPPENED?" Rose crunched her way across the living room feeling a blast of icy air from the shattered window. A black car pulled up outside their house and then Susan appeared at their door.

"Rose, Tom, are you alright?"

"I'm fine. Tom's a bit cut and dazed, but we're alright. What on earth just happened?"

"It was Jim. Jim Reynolds. He's back in town. I think that was just a warning shot. Thank God you are both alright."

Tom got up and shook tiny shards of glass from his clothing. Rose looked at his cut face.

"Tom, I think that you should go to the emergency room. Some of these pieces of glass are quite deeply embedded and will need tweezers to remove them. I'll drive you over to Goderich Hospital," Rose said feeling a bit shaky as the aftermath of what had just happened hit her.

"OH, but the window needs to be sealed otherwise we'll freeze to death," Tom answered sounding equally shaky as Rose.

Susan quickly interjected. "I've already called for an ambulance. You go together and I'll get Constable Brown to organize sealing up your window. By the time that you get back it will all be done. Now go and stop fretting about the house."

Susan watched as the Blair's put on their winter coats. Poor Tom looked a sight, but experience had taught her that facial wounds always looked worse than they were. He would be okay, of that, she was sure. But what an end to a day, Susan thought as she spoke to her constables on the phone.

A red truck matching the description of the one she had seen had been found abandoned on Orchard Line. It appeared that Jim Reynolds had eluded them once again.

ELEVEN

Susan swam up and down the swimming pool deep in thought. Henri had phoned and told her that he was finishing up some reports and would be driving down to Bayfield today. The business with Jim Reynolds had set him on red alert. He was greatly concerned for her wellbeing, although Susan still felt in her heart that Jim would never do her any harm.

Why, oh why, did he have to come back and stir up all those old feelings?

As for Henri, Susan knew that the time had come for plain talking. They were neither of them, spring chickens anymore. Both of them could retire on full pensions anytime, but the problem was with what then? Would Henri leave his beloved Montreal and move to London, or would she have to bite the bullet and move to Quebec?

When she had finished with the murder inquiry, they would have to thrash it out once and for all and then maybe make some wedding plans.

It was 8:15 before Susan pulled up in front of the Lion's

Building. The temperature had plummeted to minus twenty degrees. There was a heavy blanket of grey, cloudy sky with what looked like pink, puff balls fanning out at intervals. More snow was coming by the looks of things. That would make almost a metre of accumulated snow on the ground. Would the winter never end, Susan thought as she trudged through the churned up snowy mess of a pathway up to the hall.

The team was waiting for her. There was a general buzz in the air which came with every case when it was felt that they were getting close to breaking it. Having the Jim Reynolds distraction had proved a good morale booster for the team, Susan mused as she greeted everyone.

"Good morning. As you all know we had quite the night, but unfortunately, Jim Reynolds got away. Judging by the car tracks out on Orchard Line, it would appear that he had planned his getaway carefully. We have no idea what car he is driving but we suspect that he is headed for Wingham where his family lives. We have their house under surveillance. Now, anymore developments to report on the Joe Berry case?"

THERE WAS A STONY SILENCE, so Susan continued. "I've just received a copy of the pathologist's report on Gillian Jeffries. It appeared that she had consumed a considerable amount of whisky prior to her death. The alcohol in her blood was extremely high. The time of death has been estimated at between 11:00 p.m. on Sunday and 1:00 a.m. on Monday. Although she had been badly battered, she had not actually died of the battering. Her death was by inhalation of vomit. She drowned in her own bile.

Now we still haven't found the blunt instrument used to

kill her, but according to forensics, it would have to be a hammer or a rock, something quite heavy. We're probably looking at a male, at least six foot tall, and quite fit judging by the force and strength of the inflicted blow. We have also ruled out Cynthia as we have already established that she was in Clinton with her aunt at the time of the murder. We need to go back to the members of the band.

Constables Brown and Elliot, I want you to re-interview Adam Franks, the lead guitarist, and also John Selbrook, the drummer. Sergeant Flowers, go back to Bill Jenson and interview his family and friends. Leave no stone unturned. I also have not entirely ruled out her ex-husband, Andy Jeffries. This case is rapidly running out of steam. We need results and now."

Susan pondered the information that they had received. The fact that Gillian Jeffries had definitely known Joe Berry had done nothing to help solve the murders. If anything, it just made it all just that bit more complicated.

"By the way," Susan asked, "Did we ever get the printout from Joe Berry's cell phone? Didn't someone in the Albion say that Joe was on the phone during their dinner? Constable Elliot, can you search through the reports sent back from the Crimes Unit and see if they have already sent us the printout for Joe's cell phone? If they haven't, I want it now."

AN HOUR later Susan decided it was time to wrap up for the day. The initial buzz had been diffused and had now been replaced with a dull feeling of desperation. They appeared to be getting no closer to solving the case and everyone in the room had tangibly felt the case slipping away from them.

"Thanks everyone for coming in this morning, especially

considering that it's a Sunday and a long weekend. Let's arrange to meet again the same time tomorrow."

Susan looked at her watch. It was only eleven o'clock, far too early for lunch although she could go to the Albion and have a cup of coffee and talk to the bartender again.

She was still seething at herself for being so close to apprehending Jim, but the man had once again evaded them. Even with closing off the highway to Wingham the previous night they had not succeeded in catching him. They would catch up with him eventually, but when?

Susan parked outside The Albion. Hers was the only car on the road and once again Main Street looked like a deserted ghost town. Could she survive a winter living in Bayfield, she wondered as she entered the warmth of the Albion.

She was not the only person inside. There were two couples, obviously walkers, as they wore hiking boots and a backpack sat on the floor next to the bar. They were in deep conversation and did not acknowledge Susan entering. The bartender was busy polishing glasses. Susan looked around appreciatively at the painted mural portraying the Elliott brothers, Fred and Harvey.

The murder that had taken place in 1898 still resonated today and had become something of a folklore in the village. It was like the Black Donnelly's in Lucan. There was even a museum dedicated to that notorious family. Susan walked over to the bartender and introduced herself whilst showing her warrant card.

"Good day, I'm Detective Inspector Parker. Could I have a few words with you, please?"

He looked a little nervous, but nodded his head muttering, "Go ahead."

"Last night, there was a man of interest to us drinking

here in the bar at around 9:00 p.m. He had a thick, black beard. Did he talk to you at all other than to order a drink?"

"Yes, I remember the man. He was quiet and polite. I asked him if he was from around here and he just nodded. I took that to mean yes. Oh, he did ask about the murder, said that he was out of the country when it had happened. He wanted to know if the Serious Crimes Unit from London was handling it. That was about the extent of our conversation."

So that was how he knew I was here, Susan thought as she thanked the bartender and ordered her coffee and a sandwich.

SITTING at the table nearest to the fireplace, Susan fished out her phone. There were two messages, both from Henri. He would be in the village by about 2:00 p.m. The second message was asking Susan to book reservations at The Black Dog for the two of them for that night.

Susan laughed at the latter message. No way would she have to reserve a table. It was so quiet in the village they would be lucky if they got any customers.

ROSE SIGHED DEEPLY as she got out of bed that morning. They had been at the hospital the better part of the night. Tom had five stitches on his forehead, two on his left cheek and four on his neck. The nurse had spent an hour pulling out slivers of glass from his face, patiently using long handled tweezers. They had finally made it home at two in the morning.

It was now nine o'clock and Rose was beginning to panic about Soups On. The phone rang. It was Peggy calling from the Town Hall.

. . .

"ROSE, I just heard about the shooting. Is Tom okay?"

"Yes, Peggy, he's alright, just a few cuts on his face. I think that he was more shocked than anything else. I've left him in bed sleeping. We've got someone coming around this morning to fix the window. I must say, the police were very kind. They cleared up all the glass and taped plastic over the broken window."

"Are you still okay about making the soup for tomorrow, Rose?"

Rose knew that Peggy hated cooking and there really was no one else on the committee available to make a soup.

"YES, of course, no problem. I haven't yet decided which soup I'm going to make but don't worry, I'll be there, soup all ready. Jessica and the kids are coming up for the day so it should all be good fun."

Rose put down the phone and sighed again. She wished that she felt cheerier. She had put on a good voice on the phone, but if truth be known, she was finding the long, cold winter very depressing. She also, so missed her friend Mary. Rose shook her head and got out the ground mince from the fridge.

Her soup making plans had been somewhat interrupted by the events of last night. She decided she would go with the Italian Wedding soup. Instead of using a slow cooker as she had originally planned, she would make her soup in a saucepan and just slowly cook it on the stove top.

She fried up the onions, peppers, and garlic and added a couple of tins of tomatoes, a pint of beef stock, and then rolled little balls of ground mince in her hands. Tossing them into the boiling broth she added the pasta which always reminded Rose of rice.

Leaving the soup to simmer, she turned her mind to breakfast. It was ten before Tom appeared fully dressed and none the worse for his night-time ordeal. He went up to Rose and kissed her on her cheek.

"Hi darling. Mmm...something smells good."

"Oh, you can smell the soup, but I'm making us a frittata. Do you want a cup of tea, my love?"

Tom nodded and sat down at the table.

"Rose, did Susan tell you what the shooting was all about?"

"Yes. Jim Reynolds wanted to give us a scare. She doesn't think that it was meant to be anything but a warning to us."

"I thought that we had seen the last of the man when we spotted him in Vienna. Wow, but that really gave me a jolt."

"I know Tom. You were so lucky. Have you let the dogs out, by the way? They were both snuggled up to you on the bed. I didn't have the heart to wake them."

"Yes, they're outside right now. Looks like another cold day. What have you got on today, love?"

Rose thought for a minute. "Well, I'm meeting Peggy at the Town Hall. We're going to set up the tables for Soups On. Are you still okay with taking in the money at the door tomorrow?"

"Oh, yes, that's fine. How many participants are you expecting this year?"

"I THINK that there are about twenty-four including all the restaurants and churches. Oh, Tom, I wonder what time Jessica and the girls will be here tomorrow. I hope they know we'll be at the Town Hall from about 12:30 on. Can you give her a call while I'm out, love?"

Rose took the Frittata out of the oven and put it on the table in front of Tom. She poured out two cups of tea and sliced some fresh, crusty artisan bread.

"Here you are, my love. Eat up and then I'm out of here. I'll just let those dogs in."

Rose got up and went to the back door. Normally Ben and Puff scratched at the door to be let in, but when she opened the door, she couldn't see them anywhere. Suddenly Rose cried out.

"Tom, oh Tom, come quickly. Something's wrong with Puff and Ben. Oh… Tom, they're just lying in the snow."

Rose scrambled to put on her boots and grabbing her jacket, she ran outside to where the dogs were lying prone on the snow packed ground. They were both shallow breathing, letting out little puffs of clouds around their nostrils. Tom ran out and knelt down beside Ben.

"Oh, Benny-boy, what's happened to you, boy?"

"Tom, carry the dogs to the car. They need to get to the vet quickly. I'll phone and see if the emergency vet is available."

Tom lifted Ben up slowly. He weighed nearly eighty pounds. He staggered around the side of the house and out to where the car was parked. He opened the Volvo and laid Ben gently on a blanket at the back of the vehicle. He then returned for Puff who was considerably lighter and easier to carry than Ben. Both dogs lay side by side. Rose jumped into the car and they set off at a speed to drive to Zurich.

"Oh, Tom, what's wrong with them?" Her voice quivered and Tom reached over to grab her hand.

"Don't worry, darling, I'm sure that there's a simple

explanation. Doctor Harrison will find out what's wrong and they'll soon be right as rain."

Rose wasn't so sure. She didn't feel that optimistic at all. *Oh my gosh*, she thought, *what will we do if both dogs die?*

It took them fifteen minutes to reach Zurich. The vet was waiting with a trolley to transport the dogs into the clinic. Inside the vets building he got out his stethoscope and listened to both dog's heartbeat.

"Good strong heartbeats here which is an excellent sign." He lifted up their eyelids. "These two have been deeply sedated. If I was to hazard a guess, I would say that they have been drugged. I'll take some blood tests, but judging by their deep, shallow breathing, my guess is that they will sleep solidly for at least the next twenty-four hours. They will probably wake up none the wiser from their ordeal. More importantly, who would drug your dogs and why?"

Rose and Tom looked at each other both having the same thought. Jim Reynolds. If he could shoot at their home then he could just as easily drug their dogs, but how and when?

"YOU KNOW, the most common way animals get drugged is through peppering chunks of meat with some strong sedative. My guess is that Ben and Puff both found some tasty pieces of meat lying on the snow, probably just tossed over the fence. They would have gulped the meat down just like that." The vet snapped his fingers to illustrate.

"They'll be alright I'm sure once the sedative wears off. Leave them here for now and I'll call you just as soon as they wake up."

"Thank you, Doctor," said Rose. They both left the clinic deep in thought and drove back to Bayfield in silence.

. . .

HENRI ARRIVED at the Bayfield Village Inn earlier than he had anticipated. Susan was just pulling into the car park when she saw his black Crown Victoria parked in front of the Inn. Her heart gave a little flutter as she got out of the car and hurried into the foyer. Henri was sitting in the lounge quietly reading a newspaper. She studied him from a distance before he could acknowledge her arrival.

Henri was wearing a black leather jacket. His long, dark hair curled up against his collar. A dark shadow already framed his jaw line. Henri was one of those men who needed to shave at least twice a day otherwise the dark stubble would grow rapidly into a rough beard. He had a large nose, slightly hooked and thick, black, unruly eyebrows. Rugged, but at the same time suave and incredibly sexy, was how Susan described Henri. She walked over to where he was sitting still engrossed in the paper and wrapped her arms around his shoulders.

"Hey, you, you're early." And with that they embraced and kissed passionately. Breaking away from her embrace Henri said, "Ma Cherie. It's been too long. Let's go to your room."

They walked arm in arm to Susan's suite and closed the door behind them before putting up the 'Do Not Disturb' sign.

TWELVE

Susan left Henri sleeping. With a pang of jealousy, she'd gotten up, showered, and crept out of the bedroom without disturbing Henri. She would have loved to have stayed in bed cuddled up to Henri, but work called, and her team would be waiting.

As she pulled up outside The Lion's Hall and got out of her car, a gust of icy wind blew Susan's knitted torque off her head and she scrambled to catch it. Her hair was being blown in her face so much that by the time that she walked through the door she felt as if she had been pulled through a hedge backwards.

"Good morning everyone," Susan said to her team. "I know that it's Family Day holiday today, so I'll make this as brief as possible. We still have a murder to solve and we're not getting anywhere very fast with this one. Let us review the case.

Joe Berry was found stabbed through his neck with a newly acquired Town Hall knife. Just prior to the murder he was overheard having a heated argument with a woman we think to be Gillian Jeffries. The three band members, Bill, John, and Adam were the only people downstairs at the time of the murder. Cynthia was performing on stage upstairs. There are over one hundred eyewitnesses to that.

From the time the band last saw Joe Berry alive until he was found by Peggy Grierson, there was a time period of just twenty minutes, long enough for our killer to go into the kitchen, retrieve the knife and stab Joe through his neck. According to the interview notes, Bill left the room ostensibly to go for a quick smoke. He was gone for ten minutes. Adam also apparently left the room for five minutes while he went to the washroom. John never left the room at all. Other than the band members we have no further possible suspects.

Then we have the brutal murder of Gillian Jeffries two days later. Whereas the Town Hall murder appears to have been premeditated, this next one looks more frenzied. Are the two connected? Are we looking for one killer or two? Let's hear it from you."

Sergeant Flowers was the first to speak up. "Well, ma'am, the only band member who appeared to have a bone of contention with the deceased was Bill Branson, but his falling out with Joe was over thirty years ago so it doesn't seem feasible that he would hold a grudge for so long. The other two, Adam and John, are quite new to the group with none of the past history attached to them, so I can't see any motive for murder there either."

Constable Elliot piped up. "I interviewed John Selbrook's girlfriend, Penny Sybenga, and she really had very little to add. All she said was that John had been rehearsing every night and he seemed okay about the group. There was one thing that she said though that could be interesting, and that was, Joe had spoken about Cynthia and warned the group that she could make trouble for them. John, apparently, anticipated some sort of falling out between Joe and her."

"Thank you, Constable. Has anyone else got anything to add? What about the young bass guitarist, Adam Franks? Did anyone interview his family?"

Constable Brown coughed and then stood up whilst opening his notebook.

"It appears that Adam Franks had little time for girlfriends. His mom told me that she hadn't seen him for months. She lives in Winnipeg and since Adam joined The Berries, he hasn't had time to visit home. She sounded a bit fed up. He's their only son, and since her husband died, she's felt very lonely. But other than that, there doesn't seem to be anything untoward about our Adam."

"Thank you, Constable," Susan said. "Now it seems to me that Cynthia McArdle still appears to be somehow connected to this murder. Everything keeps pointing back to her, yet we still can't seem to find any motive or evidence.

The only way she could have been involved would have been with an accomplice. I am going to interview her again and I would like you, Sergeant Flowers, to speak to Bill Branson one more time. He was around when Joe and Cynthia were in a relationship.

CONSTABLE MATHIESON, I need to know more about Gillian Jeffries and her relationship to Joe Berry. Constables Brown and Elliot you are still on an around the clock surveillance of the Blair residence. Jim Reynolds eluded us once. He will not slip through the net a second time. Go to it, team. I have a meeting with the chief this Tuesday, which is tomorrow, and I need some results to show him."

The men all left the room quietly. Susan was just finishing off her report when Henri appeared at the doorway.

"All finished, Cherie?" he asked while walking into the room.

Susan looked up and smiled.

"Yes, Henri, all done. I'm famished. Should we go to The Albion for lunch?"

"Mais, oui ma Cherie. How did your briefing go?"

"We seem to be at an impasse. Cynthia McArdle is still our prime suspect, but she couldn't have actually murdered Joe Berry as she was performing on stage at the time of the murder."

"Maybe she had an accomplice?" Henri said while studying the photographs stuck up on the Incident Board. He was quiet for a while and then he picked up the case notes remarking. "Reading these notes, it appears that she probably still held a grudge against the victim. They went back forty years. Then Gillian Jeffries, according to these notes, also appears to be connected to the murdered man. A love triangle, mais oui?"

Susan looked at the incident board again. Having Henri view it with fresh eyes had been great. Somehow her team had not made the connection. Could it be as simple as the oldest grudge in the world, unrequited love? But who actually murdered both Joe Berry and Gillian Jeffries? She felt a stirring within, a little bubble of excitement. They were onto something tangible to pursue, a possible connection between the two women.

JESSICA PULLED up outside her parent's house. Abby and Ella were already unbuckled and out of the car before she had even turned her ignition off. The front door was flung open, and Ben and Puff ran out to greet their favourite visitors in the world. Tails wagging, they nudged up to the little girls practically knocking them over in their enthusiasm.

Giggles and laughter accompanied them into the hall where Rose and Tom stood arms outstretched to hug their family. Jessica took one look at her father and cried out.

"Oh my gosh, Dad! Just look at your face. What happened? You look as if you've just returned from a war zone."

Tom smiled and told Jessica the blatant lie that Rose and he had cooked up fully knowing that if their daughter had found out about the drive by shooting, she would have totally freaked out.

"Well, I was out playing with the dogs in the snow when I tripped on a buried log and fell flat on my face. I got splinters from the wood all stuck in my skin. It looks far worse than it is, love."

Jessica looked unsure whether or not to believe him, but thankfully Abby and Ella came running in chasing the dogs and squealing with delight.

"Puff, Ben, wait for me," wailed Abby as the dogs charged into the sunroom.

Rose came in carrying a carafe of coffee, a large plate of cupcakes, and two cups of orange juice.

"Come and sit down everyone. I've made some cupcakes especially for you two girls. Look, sit down and leave the dogs alone."

Jessica looked at her mother.

"Mom, are you alright? You sound a bit strained."

"Oh, darling, I'm fine. It's just been a busy week what with flying out to Nova Scotia and back. I've got some gorgeous photos to show you of the baby."

"Anne's posted tons of pictures of Oliver on Facebook.

He is so adorable. But Mom, what about that awful murder at the Town Hall? It's going to feel really creepy going to the Soups On knowing that someone was killed there barely a week ago."

It had not occurred to Rose that anyone might be put off going to the event because of the murder. Tom interrupted her thoughts by saying, "If anything there'll be an increase in numbers of people coming just to gawk at the scene of the crime."

"Oh, Dad, you don't really think so, do you," Jessica said looking suitably shocked.

"Well, love, that's human nature for you, gawking crime scenes always brings out the ghouls!"

Abby and Ella were busy licking off the frosting from the cupcakes. Puff and Ben sat on each side of the little girls intently watching every morsel being consumed with streams of saliva trickling from the sides of their mouths. Abby pulled off a chunk of cake and fed it to Puff while Ella did the same for Ben.

"There, Grandma, the dogs have had some cake, too. Can we have some more?"

Rose looked at Jessica before answering. She knew that her daughter tried to restrict their sugar intake.

"Well, my loves, maybe when we get back from the Soups On, Grandma will make some tea and we'll have some more cupcakes then. Right now, we should be getting ready to go to the Town Hall."

Tom looked at his watch. "It's a bit early to be going there, love. How about I run the soup down in the slow cooker and plug it in? That way it will be heating up and then we can all go down in an hours' time. I'll ask Peggy if there is anything else I can do. I know that the tables have all been set up. Sit down and relax a while."

Rose smiled and said, "Thanks, Tom. I could do with a little rest. It's bound to be crazy busy this afternoon."

TOM BUSIED himself in the kitchen pouring the soup into a slow cooker. He then carried it out to the car, came back to get his hat and gloves on, kissed Rose on her cheek and went off.

"Mom, Dad's face looks really bad. Are you sure that he's alright?"

"Yes, darling, he's fine. Now stop fussing about him and tell me about Rob and you. How are things going between you?"

Jessica looked over to where the girls were playing ball with Puff and Ben. She lowered her voice so that they couldn't hear her.

"We're doing fine, Mom, so don't you worry anymore. But I'm more concerned about my friend, Jackie, you know, my friend who adopted Jacob. Well, Jacob's now ten and he's been asking all sorts of questions about his birth parents. Jackie's finding it really hard. He seems so angry and demanding. She doesn't know what to do."

"Has she been up front and honest with him? Children will always see through lies, you know."

"Yes. Ever since he was old enough to understand, she told him that he was adopted, and that John and she loved him very much. It didn't seem to bother him before at all until now."

ROSE THOUGHT FOR A MINUTE. "He'll come around, but it must be tough for the little boy not knowing who his real parents are even though he loves his mom and dad."

"Yes, well, Jackie's booked him in to see a counsellor. Let's hope that will help."

They were interrupted by Abby wailing out loud, "That's not fair, it's my turn."

The girls were fighting over who would throw the ball next. Rose looked outside and then looked at her watch.

"Come on you two. Let's get your boots and coats on. We've got time to build a snowman before Grandpa gets back. Come along, let's get you some fresh air."

She turned to Jessica and said, "Relax, love, while you can. There's a new Cosmopolitan magazine over there. I bought it to read on the plane. Put your feet up and enjoy a bit of quiet time while I entertain these two little monkeys. "

Jessica smiled and said, "Thanks, mom."

Rose grabbed a carrot and a handful of raisins as she rounded up the girls and headed outside. The sky was a beautiful azure blue, and the snow was fairly sparkling in the winter sunshine. Big, waxy candle like icicles hung from the branches of the leafless trees. The dogs ran around in circles burying their silly heads in the snow and then chasing their own tails like mad things.

Abby and Ella grabbed handfuls of snow and started pounding the dogs causing Ben and Puff to start barking with sheer excitement. They certainly were fully recovered from their drug induced state. Rose decided not to mention the incident to Jessica.

"Come on girls, let's start rolling a big ball for the snow-man's body."

TWENTY MINUTES later a snowman sat squarely on the churned-up snow. Rose handed the carrot to Abby and the raisins to Ella.

"Now, give the snowman his nose and use the raisins to make his eyes and mouth. I'm going to wrap my scarf around his neck, and we'll go and find one of grandpa's hats to place on top of his head."

Soon the deed was done, and Abby and Ella ran back into the house to get their mother, calling out, "Mom, Mom, come and see our super snowman."

"I'm going to call him 'Fred," Abby said.

"No, not Fred, 'Snowy'!" yelled Ella.

Jessica's peace had been interrupted by the girls squabbling. Rose soon calmed them down. "Come on, everyone, grandpa's back. It's time to go to the Town Hall to try out all the delicious soups."

THE TOWN HALL was buzzing with people. The Family Day weekend was always busy in the village. Many people came to the Town Hall after the family skating session and chili at the arena.

THE TOWN HALL soup was set up on one of the end tables next to The Historical Society. They had called their soup, Baron Van Tuyll's Broth which Rose thought was rather original. The label on her soup just read, Italian Wedding Soup. Rather boring, Rose thought as she ladled out another cup. People kept coming and coming. Rose was interrupted by Jessica saying,

"I'll take over, Mom. You go around and sample some of the soups yourself. Dad has taken the girls home. I said that I would stay and help you."

Rose thanked her daughter and handed over the ladle. Looking around the room she suddenly spotted Susan and

Henri. He's a good-looking man, Rose thought as she approached them.

"Hi, Susan, Henri, have you come to sample some of Bayfield's finest soups?"

Susan smiled. "Yes, well Henri's come down for the weekend and I read about this in The Bayfield Breeze. So far, all the soups I've sampled have been absolutely delicious. However do you judge them? Where is Tom today? Henri was most concerned about the shooting."

Henri nodded and looked very serious.

"Mais oui; c'est trés sérioux. The fact that Jim Reynolds is armed deeply concerns me. The SWAT team is on alert. The whole of the KW region right up to Toronto is being watched, and we have around the clock surveillance in Wingham where his family lives. We will catch the man, do not worry."

Susan looked over at the crowds of people and then over to the stage.

"Rose, is there any other way on to the stage other than through those side doors and the back staircase?"

"Well, there is a back door that leads into a storage area. It is kept locked. That is the only other way in or out of the building. Would you like me to show you? Peggy has a key."

"Great, yes, if you don't mind. I would love to see it."

Susan and Rose left Henri sampling the soups. They went downstairs to the basement meeting room. As they passed the jail where Joe Berry was found murdered, Susan stopped dead in her tracks.

"Rose, you know where all the knives are kept. Can you show me exactly which drawer?"

"The knife that killed Joe Berry was brand new. As far as I know it was still in its package along with the receipt. I left it in there so I could claim it back off our treasurer. I thought you were told that?"

"Well, no. That means someone must have looked in the bag and taken it out deliberately to kill Joe. Not such a spontaneous act as opening a drawer and grabbing any knife at random. Can you show me where on the counter the package was left?"

Rose walked into the kitchen with Susan following in her heels. She pointed to a space on the countertop next to the fridge.

"That's where the bag was. It was in a Kulpeppers' bag. The garbage has been probably emptied since the concert."

Susan walked into the room where the band had been sitting. She sat on one of the chairs against the wall and then got up and paced the distance into the kitchen and then across the hall to the jail.

"Whoever killed Joe Berry must have followed him out here knowing full well where the knife was. Tom overheard two people arguing, didn't he?"

"Yes. He thought that it was Gillian Jeffries fighting with Joe. I passed her on the stairs, and she looked quite flushed. Her eyes looked red as if she had been crying."

"So presumably Joe did not return to the room after the fight. Whoever intended to kill him must have known that Gillian had gone back upstairs. He must have acted extremely quickly and come up upon Joe with great stealth, thrusting the knife into his neck. The timing must have been quite pivotal."

Rose nodded. Susan continued thinking out loud.

"Unless someone from the audience came down, entered the kitchen, found the knife and then proceeded to stab Joe, which I find quite unlikely, it really only leaves us with the three band members as our prime suspects. Oh, Rose, this case doesn't get any clearer, does it? Now let's see this other entrance before Henri sends in the cavalry looking for us."

Rose led the way up the first leg of the staircase to where a door faced them. Peggy had given her the key which she used to unlock the door. They entered a dark lobby with two doors set on each side opposite to each other and one straight ahead. Rose pointed to the door in front of them.

"That leads outside, and these two doors lead into storage rooms."

"So, someone with access to a key could have entered this way or, for that matter, made a quick exit. But Adam, Bill, or John would surely have noticed someone strange coming into the room. There is no duct work or trap doors in the jail that you know of, Rose?"

Rose laughed.

"Well, that would be a fine jail if it was that easy to escape. No, as far as I know, the jail is exactly what it is, a tiny six foot by six foot airless, window less room."

Susan sighed, "Oh well, it was worth a try."

They both retraced their steps upstairs where people were finally beginning to depart. The Soups On event was almost over and they would be able to go home shortly. The winners of the best soup were about to be announced. Rose held her breath. She did not think that her soup would win.

There were too many much more interesting soups in the room, although, she had tasted some of them and her soup could match them all, for taste. The Bayfield Mews were announced to be the winners of the Soup Ladle with the Town Hall Soup a close second. Susan patted Rose on her back saying," Well, done, Rose."

.   .   .

THAT NIGHT, curled up in bed with Tom gently snoring at her side, Rose went over in her mind the discussion she had with Susan about the three band members. Bill Jenson appeared to have the longest association with the deceased.

The other two were relatively new members of the band. Her mind wandered around some more and then went off in a tangent thinking about Jessica's friend and her son Jacob, and his quest to find his birth parents. Rose did the math and then shouted out loud, "I've got it. I think I know who killed Joe Berry."

Tom rolled over and sleepily said, "What did you say? Go back to sleep, love."

THIRTEEN

Jim Reynolds sat in his car watching the red brick, Ranch style house, which he had called home for over twenty years. It had been two years since he had seen his boys Alex and Dan. Although Alex and he had been communicating regularly on Facebook, Jim under the pseudonym of John Pearson. He had made Alex promise not to tell anyone, even his brother. It had been their little secret.

Just then the two boys emerged from the house, backpacks on their shoulders, thick scarves tied around their necks. They trudged along like any other teenagers, half shuffle, half slouch until they reached a bus stop where similarly clad high school students waited for their school bus. Both his sons had changed out of all recognition, Alex particularly, who, at sixteen, now looked uncommonly like Jim's own father. Dan, at fourteen, took after his mother. Janet had made it clear to the boys that she wanted nothing to do with Jim, their father, ever again. There had been little love lost between them anyway.

Jim, on the other hand, still held a burning desire for Susan Parker. This feeling had been rekindled when he had briefly seen her in Bayfield the other day.

As to those precocious, interfering Blair's, Tom and Rose, he hoped that his little warnings might have scared the smug looks off their faces. If the wife had not been so meddlesome, he might have continued working for the Montreal Mobsters and could have accumulated vast sums of money. As it was, he had managed to stash away a considerable amount which now lay invested in a Swiss bank account in Geneva.

Jim saw the yellow school bus stop and pick up the students. Only then did he drive away deep in thought.

DETECTIVE INSPECTOR SUSAN PARKER had already completed twenty lengths of the swimming pool by the time Jim had seen his sons board the school bus. After which, she had gone back to her room and woken Henri with a big kiss, to which he had responded by slowly undressing her and making sweet, tender love until Susan glanced at her watch and squealed that she would be late for work.

Henri had decided to spend one more day in Bayfield before heading back up to Montreal. They made plans to meet for lunch at The Little Inn.

SUSAN ARRIVED at The Lions Hall twenty minutes late. She walked in only to find that Sergeant Flowers had once again taken over. He was standing up pointing to the picture of Joe Berry stuck on the investigation white board.

"Right, lads, let's brainstorm. Who do you think murdered our Joe?"

Constable Brown stood up and said that he thought that

Bill Branson did it as he still held a grudge against Joe for taking his wife away from him.

NEXT CONSTABLE ELLIOT STOOD UP.

"I think that we're looking at two different perpetrators. My theory is that Gillian Jeffries killed Joe Berry and then Cynthia killed Gillian Jeffries. But don't ask me why because I haven't got a clue."

Susan stepped forward and coughed.

"Thank you, Sergeant. I actually like the idea of the two women being the murderers but like you, Constable, I am not sure of their motive."

Constable Mathieson interjected, "It could be that Cynthia found out about Joe Berry's relationship with Gillian Jeffries and in a fit of jealousy murdered her."

"But why," Susan asked, "murder the man you love? I can understand the possible act of jealousy. Crimes of passion have been committed for much less throughout the centuries, but I still cannot see the point in murdering your lover."

"BUT, ma'am, you've got it wrong. I meant that maybe Gillian Jeffries murdered Joe Berry and when Cynthia found out, she then killed Gillian."

"Well, we still are only purely speculating, but I like the way you are thinking. I still feel this whole investigation hinges on Cynthia McArdle, but we've interviewed her twice and still haven't come up with any evidence against the woman. If she is our prime suspect, she must have had an accomplice. Otherwise, how could she have killed Joe when she was on stage at the time of the murder? No, we'll have to dig a bit deeper. My gut instinct tells me that we are getting warmer and closer to the truth, but we're not there yet. Constable, did you get back to Adam Frank and manage to interview him again?"

Constable Elliot flicked through his notebook. Susan was always pleased when she saw the good, old-fashioned notebook being used. So many officers relied on technology: iPads, iPhones, and Blackberries. There was nothing wrong exactly with keeping abreast of changes, but you could always rely on writing in a notebook whereas the electronic devises required Wi-Fi connections which were not always readily available. *I'm just an old-fashioned girl at heart*, Susan thought as she began to listen to her Constable.

"Yes ma'am. I got hold of him. He had joined up with another band, The Humanists, and was playing a gig at The Yorker Night Club in Toronto. Bill Branson had also joined the same group and I believe they were singing some of The Berries old numbers.

Anyway, Adam didn't have anything further to add so I got back to his mother in Winnipeg. This time she seemed much more forthcoming. It appears that Adam was adopted. They only told him about the adoption a year ago after he received an anonymous letter claiming to be from his birth mother. Apparently, he went wild when he found out and accused them of deceiving him and denying him his true birth parents. His mother said they never knew themselves who his natural parents were only that they were from Montreal and that the mother was a single parent. Ma'am, he could be Cynthia McArdle's son?"

THE WHOLE ROOM fell silent as everyone processed the information. His age certainly did fit. If he was actually

Cynthia McArdle's son, it could open up a whole different line of inquiry.

"I'll get the Dartmouth Police to bring Cynthia back in for further questioning. Did you interview Bill Branson again? I still get the feeling that he's not telling the whole truth."

"I did speak to him, ma'am, and one thing that he said of interest was that he also had a relationship with Cynthia McArdle and that it had lasted for five years."

Susan went livid. "So, Constable, you mean to say that Bill had a long relationship with our prime suspect, and she never mentioned anything about him? Why didn't Bill come clean at the beginning when we first interviewed him? What is wrong with these people? Deception and lies have bugged this case from the beginning and I'm getting mighty tired of it.

ARRANGE TO HAVE Bill Branson brought in for questioning again. Maybe third time around, we might get the full story out of him."

"Now, what about Jim Reynolds? Have there been any more sightings of him in Huron County?"

"No, ma'am, but he switched cars and so far, we have not been able to trace either the make or colour of the car that he is now driving. The surveillance team is watching his house in Wingham and are on full alert but so far have not noticed anything suspicious going on in the neighbourhood."

"Thank you, Constable. Sergeant Flowers, I would like you to drive up to Toronto later on and bring Adam Frank back here for questioning. Someone is not telling the whole truth and we need to get to the bottom of it. Team, I feel that we are finally getting somewhere. Well, done."

Just then Susan's cell phone rang. She glanced down to see who was calling. It was Rose Blair.

"Inspector Parker speaking?"

"Oh, Susan, sorry to disturb you, I forgot that you would be at your team briefing right now. The thing is, I think that I know who your murderer is. Well, at least who might have a reasonable motive for murder. Can I pop over to speak to you?"

Susan looked at her watch. There was plenty of time before meeting Henri for lunch and she really was desperate for a cup of coffee.

"I'll come over to your house, if you don't mind. There doesn't seem to be anywhere that is open for coffee in the village. I'll be over in ten minutes if that's okay with you?"

The team dispersed and Susan collected her laptop and papers. *Trust Rose to be sleuthing again,* she thought as she made her way out into the freezing cold.

TOM AND ROSE had started their day with two phone calls. The first was from Paul, their son who lived on the other side of the world in Japan. He always phoned early in the morning as it was seven o'clock at night in Japan was seven o'clock in the morning in Canada. Rose had answered the phone.

"Oh, Paul, darling, how lovely to hear from you." She smiled as she listened to her son's voice.

"Mom, I've been offered a job at Fanshawe College as an ESL teacher. I think I'm going to take it."

"What about Atsuko? How does she feel about coming to live in Canada and what about her work?" Atsuko was a fashion designer. She was getting good recognition for her work and had recently been awarded the best designer of the year of children's clothing in Japan. Rose could not see her daughter-in-law wanting to forfeit her career in Japan and move to Canada at such a pivotal time.

Paul continued to talk. "Well… there is one problem. We have to apply for immigration and it's easier if Atsuko applies from Japan. So, Mom, I wondered if I could come and live with Dad and you just until I can get a place in London."

"WHAT ABOUT ATSUKO?" Rose said thinking to herself that she hoped that she would be coming with Paul.

"Mom, I just said that she will have to stay in Japan and apply for immigration here."

"Paul, immigration could take years. You can't mean to tell me that you and Atsuko will be separated for the whole duration?"

"No, not really. I will fly back to Japan for the summer holidays and come back here in time for the winter semester. We'll be fine. We've talked it over and both are in agreement. Atsuko's really busy designing a new line of clothes for the biggest online clothing company in Japan. We barely see each other at the moment what with my hours and her long working days. Don't worry, Mom, we're fine."

"But I do worry, my love. You shouldn't be separated. You just got married. Your father and I have been married for forty-four years and we have never been away from each other for more than a week."

"Times are different now, Mom. Anyway, would it be okay if I camp at your place for a few weeks until I get myself an apartment in London?"

"Yes, of course, darling. But when are you planning to be here? Isn't it already halfway through the semester?"

"They want me to start as soon as possible. The lecturer

just upped sticks and left the college in the lurch. I told them that I could start in a week's time."

"Wow, that's quick. Don't you have to give Toyota notice?"

It all seemed far too quick, Rose thought as she tried to process the thought that their son would be living with them again after so many years being away.

"I'm not hooked into any contract, mom. I've already handed in my notice."

"Well, then that's great news, love. How are you going to commute to London? You know that your father and I don't use the sports car in the winter, so we don't have a spare car for you to use."

Paul laughed as he said. "Mom, I'm not a student anymore. I intend to buy a car. I'll be on a pretty decent salary you know. Anyway, thanks a million. So how are things in sunny Bayfield?"

"Well, there is so much going on right now, but it will have to wait till you get here. You do remember how cold it is in the winter? Bring plenty of warm clothes and be prepared for awful travelling on icy roads."

They finished their conversation and Rose put the phone down. Talking to Paul always cheered her up. He was their youngest child and since moving to Japan they rarely saw him, although, since his marriage to Atsuko, they had seen more of him then in the past five years put together.

They had married in Japan the previous spring and then had flown to Canada for their Canadian wedding at the Town Hall. Once again, Rose was transported back to when her dear friend, Mary Stokes had been alive. She had been a fabulous cook and had helped Rose with the wedding. *Oh how I miss her*, Rose thought again. Would the grieving for her friend never stop?

. . .

TOM AND ROSE had their breakfast and then Tom went out to go pole walking with his men's group. He had woken up early that morning suddenly remembering that Doug had called the night before and asked if he was going pole walking with the guys. It hardly seemed possible that, up until just two weeks ago, Tom had been getting up most mornings at 7:30 a.m. to jog to Time for Toning. Thinking about that made Rose feel incredibly guilty.

Whilst she had not particularly liked Gillian Jeffries, absolutely no one deserved to be murdered so brutally. Still, Rose thought to herself, Tom had been really evasive when asked questions about Gillian's visit to their house when she had been away. He was obviously not telling her the whole story. Well, whatever had happened between Tom and Gillian, it surely would go to the grave with her, Rose hoped. Let sleeping dogs lie, she thought.

SHE BUSIED herself tidying up the kitchen. *I must phone Susan to give her my theory on who had murdered Joe Berry*, Rose thought. Thinking about sleeping dogs Rose decided to take Puff and Ben for a walk. She was just putting on her warm layers of clothing when the phone rang.

It was nine o'clock when she received the second call of the morning. It was from her sister Kate who lived in Kelowna, B.C. Rose glanced at her watch. Kelowna was three hours behind Ontario time so that would make it only six in the morning. Her sister was always up really early. Most mornings she ran several kilometres. Kate was in fact extremely healthy. Every year she entered the Okanagan Marathon. She always made Rose feel that she should immediately go on a diet or take up fitness.

Kate and her husband, Bob, had moved out West twenty years ago and just loved the outdoor wilderness. They had bought a hobby farm and raised llamas and alpacas. They had four daughters, three of whom were married and had moved away from the Okanogan Valley. Their youngest, Ally, was the 'accident' of the family.

Kate had thought that she was going into menopause when her menstruation had stopped at the age of forty-five. Nine months later, baby Ally was born. Now, at the age of sixty-three, their youngest was going off to university.

"ROSE," Kate shouted into the phone. Rose had never discovered why her sister did that. She wasn't hard of hearing but whenever she spoke on the phone, she raised her voice.

"Hi, Kate, it's early for you to be calling. Is everything okay?" Rose asked beginning to worry that maybe something had happened to Bob. She was very fond of her brother-in-law. He was a gentle giant of a man. At six foot four, he made Tom feel positively small in comparison.

"Oh yes, everything's fine, it's just that I wanted to talk to you before Ally gets up and before I go out on my run. Look, Ally had applied to go to Western University in London and she just got news that she has been accepted. The reason why I'm calling is that she wants to come over to Ontario for the summer and work and she wondered if she could apply for a job at The Little Inn or The Black Dog. Then, if she did get a job, could she stay with you and Tom? It would mean for the whole summer. Would that be okay with you?"

First Paul, and now his cousin, her niece, Ally. We should open up a lodge, Rose thought jokingly, but she smiled and said, "Of course we don't mind. We'd love to have Ally stay with us. How is she these days?"

Ally had been suffering from panic attacks and had missed a considerable amount of schooling. From what Rose could remember, she was a sweet girl. Tom and she had not been out West for almost five years when Ally would have been only about fourteen. Her anxiety attacks had started just after she had gone to high school, indeed just after Tom and Rose's last visit.

The two sisters chatted for a while and then Kate said, "I read in the newspaper about the murder at the Town Hall. You know I was a massive Joe Berry fan. I used to think he was amazingly handsome. Talk about a huge crush on him. I think all my friends were secretly in love with him too. If I remember rightly, you and Tom were an item then and you were just too wrapped up with each other to be interested in any of the pop stars. Tell me, Ro, what did he look like as an older man? You must have met him, I mean, before he was killed?"

"He looked a lot like George Clooney. I only spent about five minutes with The Berries. It was pretty awful, you know. The last picture I have of Joe Berry is lying dead in the old jail at the Town Hall."

"I hope that you're not getting involved with this case like you have in the past, Ro. Honestly, I've never heard of such a beautiful place like Bayfield having so many murders. There must be something in the water."

They chatted away for a while and then Kate said that she had to get going on her run and Rose said that the dogs were getting restless for their walk.

Grabbing her woolly hat and gloves she called the dogs over saying, "Fetch your leash, Ben!" Ben had only once in his life obeyed this command. He pranced up and down wagging his tail completely ignoring the command. Rose went into the kitchen and lifted the two leashes off the hook and grabbed a couple of plastic bags as she went by.

"Come on you two dafties," she said clipping the leashes onto their collars, "let's go for a quick walk."

They set off at a brisk pace. Although looking outside from the comfort and warmth of her living room it had appeared to be the perfect winter's day, once they were actually outside, it was brutally cold.

ROSE'S BREATH came out in misty cloud bursts and she could feel the insides of her nostrils freezing up. The cold didn't seem to bother the two dogs one single bit. Ben stopped every ten seconds to sniff some delectable smell and Puff just wanted to play in the snow by burying his shaggy head and nose deep into the fluffy white stuff.

They walked towards Pioneer Park and were the only signs of life on the terrace. The street did look beautiful, Rose observed, even though so many of the houses would be empty now until the Spring.

The owners would return from the South, mostly Florida or Mexico, although quite a number of residents were now going to Arizona and California for the winter. *Maybe Tom and I should think about becoming snowbirds,* Rose thought again as the idea kept becoming more appealing.

They reached Pioneer Park. Looking out over the lake was like observing a moonscape. Crater like areas dotted the frozen water and what looked like ice waves rose majestically along the shoreline. Rose shivered and clapped her hands together for warmth. It was so cold she could barely breathe. Stomping her feet and pulling her scarf up over her nose,

Rose tugged at the leashes. "Come on you two. We're going home. It's far too cold out here."

Just as she turned to go Rose spotted a group of men pole walking down Tuyll Street. She could see Tom and Doug chatting away and walking at a very brisk rate. She smiled. It was good to see Tom looking happy again.

RETURNING HOME, Rose put the kettle on for a nice cup of tea. She looked at her watch. Susan would be at her briefing. She should wait another hour before calling her. Time enough to bake a batch of cookies.

Rose gathered up her ingredients. She would make what she called her 'healthy' cookies. Butter, honey, oats, whole wheat flour, and almonds. So simple, but delicious with any beverage.

Thirty minutes later a mound of golden, crunchy cookies lay on the kitchen counter. Rose sat with a mug of steaming hot tea in her hands and fed half a cookie each to Ben and Puff. Tom would probably be at The Little Inn having coffee with his fellow pole walkers.

He wouldn't be back for a little while, Rose thought as she got out a pad of paper and began to gather her thoughts about the murder at the Town Hall. She was pretty convinced that Adam was Cynthia's son. Having heard about Jessica's friends adopted son, Jacob, and his anger and quest to find his natural parents, had sparked off Rose's own line of inquiry.

THE MATH WORKED; Adam was the right age to be Cynthia's son. The biggest question was whether Cynthia had been in collusion with Adam? She must have known that he was her son or maybe not?

That would, however, be just too much of a coincidence to have the mother and son performing at the same concert. Rose rarely believed in coincidences.

IF CYNTHIA HAD SOMEHOW ORCHESTRATED the whole 'meeting' then something must have gone horribly wrong unless it was all pre-meditated.

But what about Gillian Jeffries? Why was she killed? Did Cynthia have something to do with that? Rose felt over-whelmed by all the questions. She would have to concede defeat and leave it to the professionals to dig out the answers to all her questions. She picked up the phone to call Susan.

JIM REYNOLDS HAD SPENT the morning on the phone. Thank God for modern technology, he thought as he transferred money from his Swiss bank account directly into the TD Bank account of one Eric Dixon, pilot of the Lear Jet that he had chartered to take him and two passengers to Antigua. While he had his iPhone out, he decided to send a little farewell note to Susan.

He had come to realize, too late, that she had been the love of his life. Having done that, the next stop was to be a quick shop at Walmart. He would buy a suitcase and some summer wear. He could not wait to be away from Canada and the dreadful weather.

If Jim was absolutely honest with himself, he was just a bit tired of being on the run. Antigua would give him a well-deserved rest and time to bond with his family. He just hoped that Alex hadn't got cold feet.

He looked at his watch again. One more hour until he would be back in Wingham and in front of his old house, ready to pick up both the boys.

He glanced down at the three passports sitting on the passenger seat next to him. Since being on the run he had collected four different aliases. Obtaining forged passports was easy in Istanbul providing you had enough money. Corruption and bribery were, after all, the Eastern way of doing business.

HE WAS GOING to travel under the name of John Ryan the 'so called' uncle of the two boys, Alex and Dan. His whole plan relied on the speed of execution. If he could be on the plane before any alarm bells went off, they would stand a good chance of eluding the authorities.

ERIC DIXON HAD POSTED his flight plan and had told Jim that they would be landing at a small airstrip on the North side of the Island where, with a generous payment, the customs officers would turn a blind eye to the occupants of the Lear Jet.

He drove towards his old neighbourhood. Janet would be at work, but, as an added precaution, Jim had shaved off his bushy beard and dyed his hair bleached blond. He did look quite different, in fact, he wondered if Alex and Dan would even recognize their father. Thinking of the boys, Jim wondered how Dan would react to the fact that he was going away with him. Alex had already acknowledged that he was pretty cool with everything, but Dan was much more of a 'mother's boy.'

· · ·

JIM EXPECTED some resistance from Dan. He hoped that he would not have to resort to 'kidnapping' his own son. Shaking his head and trying to move on to more pleasant thoughts, Jim contemplated his plans to purchase a beach resort that he had seen advertised on Craig's List. He had already made some enquiries. The price was right. It needed some upgrading, but the boys could help with that. Between them they could run the resort together and have a good life in the sun. That was his plan and he intended to keep to it.

Jim looked at his watch again. It was almost 2:35 p.m. The boys would be getting off the school bus any minute now. It was then that Jim spotted the unmarked police car. *Damn,* he thought, *I'll have to circle around the block again.*

THE POLICE SURVEILLANCE TEAM HAD, in fact, noticed the blue Honda Civic but the description of the driver did not match that of Jim Reynolds. They watched the car for a while and then it drove away just as the yellow school bus pulled up alongside the sidewalk and the two Reynolds boys alighted from the bus. From a distance it appeared that the brothers were in deep conversation.

The officers watched them for a while and then drove off to drive the circuit that would take them around the block and back again.

JIM REYNOLDS PULLED into a side road and waited a few minutes before doubling back to where the boys were now only a few metres from their house. He idled his car alongside the sidewalk and opened the passenger window.

"Alex, Dan, get in the car quickly."

Alex opened the back passenger door and fairly pushed

his younger brother into the car, slamming the door behind him.

"Let's go, dad."

And with that Jim pulled away from the curb and hit the accelerator. It was 2:45 p.m. They had less than one hour to get to Centralia and be aboard the plane to take them to the Caribbean.

CONSTABLE BROWN CALLED Susan and announced that he had Bill Branson in the car. He had picked him up early that morning from London and had offered to drive him back after the interview. Bill didn't drive so he had no way of getting out to Bayfield. The Constable had tracked him down at The Yorker Night Club where he had been playing with another group, The Caraway's, the previous evening.

"Should I bring him in now, ma'am," The Constable asked glancing at his watch.

Susan looked up from the report that she had been writing and nodded her head.

"Yes, thank you, Constable. Let's get this over with so that you can drive him back to London."

BILL BRANSON WALKED into the room looking some-what worse for wear. His eyes were bloodshot, and his clothes looked as if he had slept in them. He stopped in front of the white board which held some very gory pictures of both Gillian and Joe's dead bodies. Along with the murdered victims there were pictures of the band members and Cynthia. Down on the bottom right of the white board was a photograph of Jim Reynolds.

"Come and sit down, Bill. Now, I see that you have not

exactly been crystal clear with the facts. Could I remind you that you have wasted our time by not telling us the truth? I need to caution you that you could be charged with holding back vital evidence in a murder investigation. Now, tell us about your relationship with Cynthia McArdle and do not obstruct the case anymore by leaving anything out." Susan said having decided to take a hard line with Bill Branson.

Bill looked as if all the wind had been taken out of his sails. He coughed and then blew his nose loudly, then began to talk.

"I got to know Cynthia quite well when she was dating Joe. To be honest, I thought that he treated her badly by dumping her the way he did. I know she was a bit obsessional and, sure, the stalking was weird, but she loved the guy, and that was the plain truth of the matter. Anyhow, I never saw or heard from her again for about five years and then, out of the blue, I bumped into her at a concert. By then The Berries had split up and I was in a downward spiral of self-pity and disgust. Cynthia helped me get back on my feet. We actually had some good times together. It all went belly up when I discovered that she was still in love with Joe even after he had married Jenny. We split up and shortly after that Joe approached me and we reformed The Berries. The rest of the story is history."

"So why did you pretend to not know Cynthia when she arrived at the Town Hall. You must have recognized her?"

"To be quite honest at first I did not recognize her at all. It had been over twenty years and we both had changed considerably. I also wanted to let sleeping dogs lie. No way did I want to strike up another relationship with her. She is one unstable lady, spiteful and mean when she wants to be, so, no way did I want to get anywhere near Cynthia McArdle ever again."

"And what about Joe, surely he must have recognized her?"

"Joe found everything a big laugh, a joke. He was probably pissing himself at seeing the stalker, as he used to call her, so innocently playing at his gig. No, Joe knew what was going on. He was just playing along with the game."

"Did he even talk to Cynthia downstairs at the Town Hall?"

"No. I caught him winking at her just as she was going upstairs to perform. He rolled his eyes at me too, so I knew what he was up to. As I said, he was playing games, that's all."

Games that probably cost him his life, Susan thought as she wrapped up the interview and thanked Bill for coming in.

She decided to dismiss the team early. Rose had called and she needed to go and speak to her quite urgently.

TEN MINUTES later Susan was sitting at the kitchen table while Rose busied herself with putting a carafe of coffee on the tray and placing cookies on a plate. She looked around the lovely room and could see that it truly was a working kitchen. Flour and sugar canisters stood on the granite countertop alongside an olive oil jug. Photographs of gap-toothed grandchildren adorned the stainless-steel fridge. Ben and Puff lay at Rose's feet sound asleep.

"Here you are," Rose said as she poured out the coffee and lifted the plate of cookies on to the table.

"So, Rose, tell me who you think murdered Joe Berry."

Susan smiled as she spoke. Rose had always amazed her with her perception and her tenacity to solve a problem. Even at university, her friend had never given up on anything. She was like a dog with an old bone once she got her teeth into a project. Rose looked at Susan and then pulled out a folded sheet of paper from her pocket.

"I sat down this morning and wrote down my thoughts, but I'm afraid that I still have too many questions and not enough answers. You see, I think that Adam Frank is Cynthia McArdle's son. His age fits and he was born in Montreal and was adopted. Those are all facts, undisputed facts. What I think happened, but I seem to have no real proof, is I think Adam somehow confronted his father, Joe, and in a fit of rage, killed him. I reckon Cynthia told him beforehand that Joe was his father and that sent him into a rage.

As to Gillian Jeffries, well, maybe Adam overheard the argument between Joe and Gillian and in doing so, whatever she said must have sealed her own fate. But, Susan, this is all pure conjecture. I might be horribly wrong. What do you think?"

Susan laughed out loud. "Rose, you have pretty well come to the same conclusions as our team did this morning at our meeting. I will be interviewing Cynthia McArdle again this afternoon. Hopefully, this time she might tell us the whole truth and we might have some answers by tomorrow."

Rose never got to answer her friend because Susan's cell phone started to ring.

"Inspector Parker speaking," Susan answered crisply.

Rose could see Susan's lovely face cloud over as she said, "Yes, yes, I'll join you in a few minutes. I'll alert the team. Thanks Henri." Susan put her phone away and turned to Rose.

"Sorry, Rose, I have to go. Our friend Jim Reynolds has been spotted. The surveillance team were just reviewing the camera footage when they noticed a blue Honda Civic which had driven around the block and then pulled up alongside the Reynolds boys. Jim has taken his sons in the car with him and is currently heading towards Clinton. The O.P.P. have been alerted. Henri and I are going to try to intercept him and attempt to make him give himself and the boys up before more harm is done."

"Oh, my, gosh, Susan. Be careful. After what Jim did to us, he could be really dangerous."

Rose looked worried. Her face scrunched up with concern.

Susan tried to reassure her friend. "Don't worry, Rose. One way or another we will put an end to Jim's flight. But right now, I do need to dash. Hopefully I'll be back in time to interview Cynthia, if not, our friends from Dartmouth Police will have to do the job for me. I will be around to speak to Adam, I hope, and I'll let you know of the outcome."

"Here, Susan, take some cookies for you and Henri to eat in the car. It looks as if you'll be skipping lunch."

Susan left quickly leaving Rose deep in thought. She had only been gone about five minutes when Rose noticed a small black, pocket-sized wallet on the sofa. It was Susan's. She had accidently left her wallet behind. Rose picked up her phone and dialed Susan's cell number.

IN DARTMOUTH, a very angry Cynthia sat chewing her nails in the small interview room. She periodically looked up and glanced around the room furtively, her eyes darting around like a crazy chameleon. Her heart had sunk when she had received the phone call from the police. Deep inside she just knew that it was all over. Her plan to reunite her long, lost son with his father had all gone belly up and it was all her fault. When she had finally found Adam after all those years, it had been like a miracle come true.

Her baby. It had been the most amazing part of her life

being reunited with him, until he had started pestering her for information about his 'real' dad. She should never have raged on about how Joe had abandoned her, leaving her no choice but to have the baby, her darling baby, put up for adoption.

She had told him how it had broken her heart. Her life had been totally destroyed. Of course, if she had been at all truthful, she had to say that she had somewhat over dramatized it all. She wasn't to know the pent-up anger and rage that had consumed and built up in Adam. It was Cynthia who had suggested that he confront his father. But she wanted to be there when he did. Instead, he must have told Joe that he was his son when she was on stage performing. How was she to know that he would stab Joe to death?

Cynthia waited and waited, steadily getting more and more pumped up with self-indignation. None of this had been her fault. How dare they treat her like some common criminal?

Finally, Detective Harrington appeared at the door.

"It appears that Inspector Parker has been detained. I will conduct the interview myself. May I remind you that whatever you say may be taken down and used in court..."

Cynthia snarled and then started to scream like a wild banshee.

SUSAN SAT in the passenger seat of Henri's black Crown Royal. "Cherie, the blue Honda is now on Highway 4 heading towards Vanastra. It is my guess that he is heading towards London. If we head up to Brucefield we won't be that far behind him. A general APB has gone out to all cruisers in the area."

They drove on in silence past Varna, then turned right at

Brucefield, and onto Highway 4. Exeter was fifteen minutes away, but Henri managed to drive there in ten minutes causing Susan to hold her breath and cling desperately to the sides of her seat. Every time Henri overtook a vehicle, she held her breath again and closed her eyes. He was driving like a mad man.

Susan's phone rang shrilly. The minute that Susan felt in her pocket for her phone she also realized that her wallet was missing. She saw on the cell's display that it was Rose.

"Hi, Rose, I know exactly what you're going to tell me." She was about to continue when the police radio crackled out.

"Blue Honda seen turning right on to Victoria Street."

Susan thought quickly. Victoria Street took you up to Centralia, the old air force base. There still was a privately owned airport and good runway in Centralia.

"Henri, I think I know where Jim is heading. He must have chartered an aircraft out of Centralia. I'll get a hold of the base and see who is on the manifest to fly out today."

Rose could hear the whole conversation between Henri and Susan. She waited for Susan to continue their conversation.

"Oh, Rose, sorry about that. Look, I have to go now. I'll pick the wallet up later on. Bye."

With that Susan scrolled through her iPhone until she found the right number. Soon she was talking to the flight planner at Centralia. He confirmed that a John Ryan and his two 'nephews' were booked to fly to Antigua in a Lear Jet, owned and operated by Eric Dixon.

They were closing in on Jim, Susan thought as Henri turned right on Victoria and drove like a man possessed towards Centralia. They could only be a few minutes behind him now.

Susan got out her phone and contacted the Dartmouth Police. They would have to conduct the interview without her. She noticed that there was one message in her mailbox. She opened it and gasped. It was from Jim Reynolds.

Susie, I just wanted you to know that I am so very sorry for everything. I realize now that what we shared together was precious. I will always remember our time together. I love you.
Jim

"MA CHERIE, WHAT IS WRONG?" Henri said still speeding like a mad man but now obviously concerned by Susan's reaction to her message.

"Um…it's nothing, Henri. Look, look over there. Isn't that the blue Honda?"

OVER BY THE old airport buildings a car was parked. Jim, with his two boys, were running towards a small, white Lear Jet.

Henri pushed his foot hard on the accelerator. They raced over towards the plane just screeching to a halt behind Jim and the boys. Henri and Susan leapt out of the car. Henri called out. "Stop!"

Jim pushed his boys and their suitcases towards the plane. He then pulled out a gun.

"No, I suggest that you stop and stay right where you are. I will shoot if you move any closer."

Alex turned his head and saw his father holding the gun in his hand.

"Dad, Dad, what are you doing with that gun?"

"Son, just get on the plane with Dan. I'll join you in a minute. Tell the pilot to start up the engine."

ROSE HAD NOT BEEN able to relax at all since her conversation with Susan. When Tom came in from pole walking, she was beside herself with worry. Sometimes, Rose felt that she had been born with a sixth sense.

Right now, her senses were telling her that her friend needed her and that something very bad was about to happen.

"Tom, will you come with me. Susan left her wallet behind, and Jim Reynolds has taken his boys, and I know where they're all going. Oh, Tom, something really bad is going to happen."

"Rose, love, whatever are you talking about. Slow down and tell me again slowly. You look so agitated."

Rose took a deep breath and explained to Tom what had happened and what she had overheard on the phone.

"So, you see, Tom, I reckon he's heading for the airport at Centralia. Oh, Tom I just feel it in my bones that something dreadful is going to happen. I have to go and warn Susan. Please, please, drive me to Centralia."

They set off five minutes later against Tom's better judgement. The clear blue sky of the morning had been replaced with rather ominous grey, pink tinged clouds. Snow was on its way, of that Tom was sure. Driving through Varna towards Brucefield Rose urged Tom to drive faster.

"Take Airport Road, Tom, it will save us driving through Exeter and we'll make up some time as well."

Tom glanced at his wife. She could be so bossy sometimes, particularly when she was stressed out.

"Calm down, love. We'll get there in good time."

Rose kept thinking of Jim Reynolds and how he obviously had no conscience. If he could shoot blindly at Tom and drug their dogs, he would stop at nothing. *Please*, she thought, *please be careful Susan.*

ADAM FRANKS HAD BEEN CONTACTED and brought in for questioning. Sergeant Flowers, in the absence of Inspector Parker, conducted the interview. The guitarist sat in the interview room in a sulky silence. He was a handsome young man with thick, curly auburn, almost red, hair worn shoulder length. He had a freckled face that made him look much younger than his thirty-four years.

"Right. I need to firstly remind you of your rights. Whatever you do or say will be recorded and will be held in evidence against you. If you feel that you require a solicitor, then now's the time to say so."

The Sergeant looked at Adam Frank who was still sitting there impassively.

"Okay. We need to record the basic facts again for the records. Your first and last name please."

Adam coughed and shrugged his shoulders.

"Adam John Frank."

"Date of birth," The Sergeant continued.

"August 6, 1980."

"Place of birth."

"Montreal."

"Is it true that you were adopted by Julie and Bob Frank and grew up in Winnipeg?"

"Yes, that is correct."

"Do you know who your birth mother is?"

"Yes. Her name is Cynthia McArdle."

"When did you discover the name of your birth mother?"

Adam paused for a minute before saying, "Five years ago I received a letter from Cynthia. She told me that she had spent years trying to find me. She told me everything. Who my real father was and everything about him."

"Who is your birth father?" The Sergeant asked trying to keep an even voice.

Adam went very quiet and hung his head down low. Sergeant Flowers repeated the question one more time.

"Umm…my father was Joe Berry."

"Did you kill Joe Berry?"

Once again Adam paused and then he threw his head back defiantly. This time his voice took on a different tone as he shouted, "Yes. Yes, I did kill the lying bastard. He was my father and he tried denying it. After all this time and all my careful planning, he flatly denied that I was his son."

Sergeant Flowers calmly said, "No need to shout. Take it from the beginning and explain what happened."

Adam took a deep breath and seemed to visibly calm down.

"Well, after I got the letter from my mother, I planned it all. I managed to get the position as lead guitarist in the band. Of course, Joe didn't know who I was. I actually quite liked playing with The Berries and my parents thought that it was really cool. I got to know my father quite well over the years. I realized that he was a philandering bastard, always cheating on his wife Jenny. I met up with Cynthia, my real mom, several times and we planned a time when we all three would be together. Cynthia made me promise not to tell Joe that I was his son before she could be there to watch his reaction to the news. Finally, she managed to get the gig as supporting artist here in Bayfield."

Sergeant Flowers interrupted Adam.

"So let me get this straight. Cynthia McArdle and you planned this together?"

Adam coughed again.

"Well, not exactly. The big plan was to reunite my parents, but it all misfired. When I went to tell Joe that I was his son, he was in the middle of an argument with that slut, Gillian Jeffries. My mom told me about her and how my dad had a relationship with her. It was because of that bitch my dad dropped my mom. I overheard her say she still loved him. What right had she to say that?"

Adam fidgeted with his 'T' shirt, tucking it in to his jeans and then pulling it out again. Seeing Sergeant Flowers serious face he reluctantly decided to continue.

"When I saw him standing there smirking to himself after she left him I felt such an urge to kill him. I went into the kitchen and saw the bag containing the knife. I grabbed it and without stopping to think I charged into the hallway. I came up behind Joe and dragged him into the small room that I later found out was called the jail. It was so quick. I didn't have time to think."

Adam paused again and took a deep gulp of air before continuing,

"One minute he was standing there with his back to me and the next I had thrust the knife through his throat. I pushed him into the jail and walked out. I didn't even stop to see the damage. I presumed that Joe Berry was dead. I walked to the washroom, washed my hands and went back into the back room. It was all over and done within five minutes."

Sergeant Flowers interrupted him again.

"So, what about Gillian Jeffries? Why did you have to murder her?"

Adam went quiet for what seemed like an eternity and then he spoke softly, all defiance removed from his voice.

"After I killed my father and realized that my real mother, Cynthia, would never be reunited with her first love, it made me so angry to think of Gillian Jeffries and how she had been obviously dating my father. The silly bitch thought nobody knew what they were up to, sneaking around, and stalking Joe like a crazed groupie.

WHEN I OVERHEARD THEM ARGUING, I decided there and then that she needed to be purged from this earth."

Again, Adam paused, but this time he looked contrite and continued with almost a whisper.

"To be honest, I don't know why I did it, but I just did, and it was easy, too easy. She even let me in and welcomed me. The worse thing of all was that she actually started flirting with me. She was wearing black, silky pyjamas which showed every curve in her body. She sat down at her computer to turn it off and I just grabbed the first thing that I could find. It was a large painted rock sitting on the shelf above her desk. I smashed the back of her head in. Good riddance is what I thought."

Adam looked thoughtful and cocked his head to one side like a little sparrow. He continued with almost a monotone voice.

"YOU KNOW, Sergeant, what they say about killing. The first time is the hardest and after that it is plain and simply easy."

"What did you do with the painted rock?"

"I threw it in the river. It broke through the ice and now lies at the bottom of the Bayfield River."

The defiance was returning, and Adam started to rock

himself back and forward as he built up a self-induced fury to the way he perceived that he had been treated.

"They both deserved to die. They were just the scum of the earth."

Sergeant Flowers looked at Adam with ill-concealed disgust. The young man was clearly deranged. He pulled out his arrest warrant card and read Adam his rights.

"Adam Frank, I am arresting you for the murders of Joe Berry and Gillian Jeffries. It is my duty to inform you that you have the right to retain and instruct counsel of your choice in private and without delay. Before you decide to answer any questions concerning this investigation, you may call a lawyer of your choice or get free advice from Duty Counsel. If you wish to contact Legal Aid Duty Counsel, I can provide you with a telephone number and a telephone will be made available to you."

Sergeant Flowers took a short breath before continuing

"You do not have to say anything unless you wish to do so. You have nothing to hope from any promise of favour and nothing to fear from any threat whether or not you say anything. Anything you say may be used as evidence. Do you understand?"

Adam nodded and, with that, Sergeant Flowers drew out his hand cuffs and strapped them around Adam Frank's wrists. He would drive him personally to London where he would be officially arraigned before appearing in court.

HENRI AND SUSAN could hear the police car sirens that had been called up for back up. The sounds got louder and louder as they got nearer. Jim stood with his gun pointed directly at Henri's chest.

"One step closer and I will shoot." He warned.

Susan called out to him.

"Jim, this won't end well. Give yourself up and let your boys go home to their mother. Don't be such a fool."

Jim looked at her and smiled. "You know, Susan, this is ironic, your boyfriend against me. Did I ever tell you how great you were in bed? Really hot. Oh, I can see by your boyfriend's face that he didn't know about our special relationship? Take it from me, Henri, you've got one hot babe there."

Susan could see Henri visibly flinch. His fists clenched as if he wanted to punch Jim in the face.

"Don't," she whispered, "he's just provoking you."

Jim continued his taunting.

"I tell you what, Susie, why don't you come with me and the boys. Could I not tempt you with the Caribbean?"

The loud sirens and flashing lights of the police cars had finally arrived. The airfield was a blaze with the flashing lights.

Jim looked nervously around. He was an open target for a sniper shot.

"I'm going to board the plane now, but if anyone moves, your lover boy here will get the first bullet through his chest."

Jim started to back away towards the Lear jet. The turbine engines were fired and roaring to go. He had just reached the steps when Henri, like a charging bull, did what to the onlookers looked like as a Rugby tackle. He fairly threw himself at Jim. At the same time as he hurdled himself through the air, a thunderous gun shot was heard. Henri's body jolted mid-air and landed heavily on the ground. Jim ran up the steps and slammed the doors of the jet shut behind him. The Lear jet started to move.

What followed looked like a well-orchestrated dance. Six

police cruisers drove at full speed alongside and in front of the jet. The plane was forced to stop.

ROSE AND TOM had witnessed the police cars chasing and stopping the plane. They did not know about the shooting until, as they approached the airport runway, they could see Susan crouched over a body lying on the tarmac.

Rose jumped out of the car and ran over to her friend.

Susan had Henri cradled in her arms. A dark pool of blood surrounded them. Henri's eyes were closed, and his skin was totally drained of all colour.

"Is he…dead?" Rose whispered to Tom who had run up to join her.

Susan turned and looked at her Rose through glazed eyes.

"Rose, what on earth are you doing here?"

"Oh, Susan, I had this terrible premonition that you were in trouble. Oh, my dear friend…"

Rose was choked for words as Tom came and put his arm around her and pulled her away.

"Leave them alone, love, leave them."

Rose and Tom walked away leaving Susan rocking Henri gently in her arms while softly crying.

THE AMBULANCE SIREN blared out loudly, lights flashing as it pulled up alongside Susan and Henri. Two paramedics jumped out and ran over and started to work on Henri. Susan stood up and, as if in a trance, she walked slowly over towards her friend, Rose.

"Oh, Rose, I think he's dead. Henri is dead…"

ACKNOWLEDGMENTS

Any errors and omissions of a historical or factual nature are mine, and for this I humbly apologize.

I would like to thank my friends who read and edited, namely Margo and Rita, and my long-suffering husband, Philip, for his support and patience during the process of writing and editing this, my third Rose Blair Murder Mystery novel.

I would also like to extend my thanks to Gary and Rita for submitting photographs of the Bayfield Town Hall for the cover. Both of you are superb photographers. I had to choose just one of them but thank you both.

Lastly, I would like to thank all the members of the Town Hall committee who work so hard to bring events like Soups On to the village. You are all great!

ROSE BLAIR'S RECIPES

Some of Rose's favourite soups

Leek and Potato Soup

Ingredients
2 tablespoons butter
2-3 cloves of garlic
3 large leeks, outside leaves disregarded
4-5 potatoes
Fresh or dried parsley
3-4 cups of stock
¾ cup plain yoghurt
2 tablespoons grated cheese

Method
Melt butter, add garlic and leeks, and stir cooking for 2-3 minutes. Add chopped potatoes, stock, and herbs plus seasoning. Bring to a boil, then simmer, and cover the pan for 25 minutes. Remove from heat, let cool for 10 minutes. Transfer half of the soup into blender or food processor and zap until smooth. Return the blended soup to the saucepan along with the unblended broth and add yoghurt and seasoning. Before serving stir in the grated cheese. Ladle into bowls and garnish with parsley.

Pea and Mint Soup

Ingredients
1 tablespoon butter
3 small onions
2 leeks, trimmed and chopped
1 potato
450g frozen peas
2 tablespoons fresh mint
3 cups stock
Fresh mint to garnish

Method
Melt butter, add onions, and cook for a couple of minutes. Add the leeks and cook a few minutes. Add potato, peas, mint, stock, and seasoning. Bring to a boil, then reduce the heat and simmer for 30 minutes. Leave it to cool for ten minutes. Blend until smooth, return it to the pan and reheat. Pour into bowls and garnish with sprigs of mint.

Carrot and Parsnip soup

Ingredients
4 tablespoons butter
1 large onion
4 carrots, peeled and chopped

2 large parsnips, peeled and chopped
1 tablespoon freshly grated ginger
1 teaspoon grated orange zest
3 cups stock
½ cup light cream (evaporated milk will do)
salt and pepper

Method

Melt butter, add chopped onion, and cook for 3 minutes. Add chopped carrots and parsnips, cover the pan, and simmer for 15 minutes until the vegetables have softened. Stir in ginger, orange zest, and stock. Bring it to a boil, reduce heat, cover the pan, and simmer for 30 minutes. Leave it for ten minutes to cool then blend until smooth. Return soup to the pan, add cream and seasoning, and warm gently over low heat. Ladle into bowls and garnish with a swirl of cream.

Mushroom and Sherry soup

Ingredients

4 tablespoons butter
2 cloves garlic
3 onions
450g mushrooms sliced
3 tablespoons chopped parsley
2 cups stock
3 tablespoons flour
½ cup milk
2 tablespoons sherry
½ cup sour cream

Method

Melt butter in pan, add garlic and onions, and cook for 3 minutes. Add mushrooms and cook for another 5 minutes. Add parsley, stock, and seasoning. Bring to a boil, simmer, cover pan, and cook for 20 minutes.

Put flour in bowl, mix enough milk to make a paste, and gently stir into the soup to thicken. Cook a further 5 minutes stirring all the time. Add remaining milk and sherry and cook for another 5 minutes. Remove from heat and stir in sour cream. Ladle into bowls and garnish with parsley.

Lemon and Asparagus Soup

Ingredients

2 tablespoons butter
3 leeks, trimmed and sliced
1 celery stalk
5 cups stock
1 tablespoon lemon zest
2 tablespoons lemon juice
1 potato, peeled and chopped
1 tablespoon chopped parsley
seasoning
450g asparagus, cut into 1 inch size pieces
½ cup light cream

Method

Melt butter, add leeks, and cook for 3 minutes. Add celery and cook another 3 minutes. Add stock, lemon zest, potato, and parsley, bring to a boil, reduce the heat, and simmer for 25 minutes. Add asparagus and cook for a further 5 minutes. Leave to cool. Blend half of the soup until smooth. Return it to the pan with the rest of the soup, stir in cream and reheat gently.

Serve with finely cut strips of lemon zest.

Sweet Potato and Stilton Soup

Ingredients
4 tablespoons butter
1 onion
2 leeks, trimmed, sliced
2 sweet potatoes, peeled and diced
4 cups stock
1 tablespoon parsley
2/3 cup heavy cream or plain yoghurt
150g Stilton cheese crumbled
2 tablespoons crumbled Stilton for garnishing

Method
Melt butter, add onion and leeks, and cook for 3 minutes. Add sweet potatoes and cook for another 5 minutes, pour in stock, and add parsley and seasoning. Bring to a boil, simmer, and cover pan for about 30 minutes. Remove from heat, leave to cool for 10 minutes. Transfer half of the soup into blender, blend until smooth, return to the remaining soup, add cream, and gradually stir in crumbled stilton until melted. Do not let the soup boil. Ladle into bowls and garnish with crumbled stilton.

Cream of Chicken Soup

Ingredients
3 tablespoons butter
1 onion, chopped
1 leek, trimmed and sliced

2 skinless, boned chicken breasts, chopped
3 cups stock
1teaspoon chopped parsley, fresh thyme
1 cup cream or yoghurt

Method

Melt butter, add onion, and cook until soft. Add leek, chicken, stock, herbs, and seasoning and bring to the boil. Simmer for 25 minutes until chicken is tender. Remove from heat and leave it to cool for 10 minutes. Blend the soup in processor until smooth. Return soup to pan and stir in cream. Gently heat soup and serve garnishing with sprigs of thyme.

Cheese and Bacon Soup

Ingredients

2 tablespoons butter
2 cloves garlic
1 onion, chopped
250g cut lean bacon
2 leeks, trimmed and sliced
2 tablespoons flour
4 cups stock
5 potatoes peeled and chopped
Seasoning
½ cup cream
3 cups grated cheese

Method

Melt butter, add garlic and onion, and cook for 3 minutes in a pan, stirring all the time. Add chopped bacon and leeks and cook for a further 3 minutes. In a bowl, mix flour with enough stock to make a paste, add to pan, stir until blended, and add stock and potatoes. Bring to a boil, then simmer for 25 minutes until potatoes are tender. Stir in cream and then gradually stir in cheese until melted. Serve garnished with grated cheese.

Spicy Lentil Soup

Ingredients
1 tablespoon olive oil
1 chopped onion
1 leek, sliced and trimmed
5 cups stock
1 carrot, peeled and chopped
1 celery stalk, chopped
1/3 cup rice
1 cup red lentils
1 tablespoon chopped parsley
Pinch of saffron
1 teaspoon coriander
1 teaspoon garam marsala
Seasoning

Method
Heat oil, add onions, and cook until softened. Add leek, cook for another two minutes, and add stock, carrots, celery, rice, lentils, and spices. Bring to a boil, then lower and simmer for 40 minutes until rice and vegetables are all cooked. Ladle into bowls and garnish with sprigs of fresh cilantro.

Pea and Ham Soup

Ingredients
1 tablespoon butter
1 onion
1 leek, sliced
4 cups stock
450g frozen or fresh peas
200g smoked ham, chopped
1 tablespoon tarragon
4 tablespoons cream or yoghurt

Method
Melt butter, add onion, and cook until softened. Add leeks, stir in stock, ham, peas, and tarragon, season, and bring to the boil, then simmer for 30 minutes.

Transfer half of the soup to a blender, blend smoothly, return it to the remaining soup. Stir in cream and cook over low heat for another 5 minutes.

Minestrone

Ingredients
2 tablespoons olive oil
2 cloves garlic
2 red onions
75g prosciutto sliced (substitute bacon if desired)
1 red pepper, chopped
1 can tomatoes
4 cups stock
1 celery stalk, chopped
1 can Borlotti beans, drained
100g shredded cabbage
75g frozen peas

1 tablespoon fresh parsley
Seasoning
75g dried vermicelli
Parmesan cheese for garnishing

Method

Heat oil, add garlic and onions, and cook until softened. Add red pepper and chopped tomatoes, stir in stock, and add celery, beans, cabbage, peas, and parsley. Season, bring to a boil, lower the heat, and cook for 30 minutes. Add vermicelli and cook for another 10 minutes or until vermicelli is cooked. Ladle into bowls and add grated parmesan.

Beef and Tomato Soup

Ingredients

3 tablespoons oil
1 onion, chopped
1 clove of garlic
2 fresh chillies finely chopped
4 large tomatoes, chopped
450g ground beef
2 carrots peeled and chopped
2 potatoes peeled and chopped
1-2 tablespoons fresh parsley
5 cups stock
Seasoning

Method

Heat oil in pan, add onions and garlic, and cook over low heat until transparent. Stir in chillies and tomatoes, add ground mince, increase heat, and brown for 5-8 minutes. Stir in carrots, potatoes, parsley, and stock. Bring it to a boil, reduce the heat, and cover. Simmer for 30 minutes or until the vegetables are tender.

Chilled Spinach and Cheese Soup

Ingredients
8oz fresh baby spinach leaves
3 cups milk
3 cups stock
1 cup cream cheese preferably garlic and herb cream cheese
Seasoning

Method
Put spinach in a pan with milk and stock. Bring it to a boil, reduce, and simmer gently for 10 minutes.

Remove from heat and let cool completely. Put soup in blender and process until smooth. Add cream cheese to broth and process again until thick and creamy. Pour soup into a bowl, season, cover with plastic wrap, and let chill in fridge for several hours. Stir well before serving. Add croutons and serve immediately.

Tuscan Bean Soup

Ingredients
300g canned cannellini beans, drained and rinsed
300g can cranberry beans (kidney beans will do)
3 cups stock
4oz small pasta shapes
4 tablespoons olive oil

2 garlic cloves
Parsley
Seasoning

Method

Put half the beans in processor with half the stock and blend until smooth. Pour into pan and add remaining beans and stock. Add pasta and return it to a boil, reduce heat, and simmer until pasta is tender. In a small pan add oil and fry garlic until tender, add to soup. Season and garnish with parsley.

A SNEAK PEEK AT MURDER AT THE MARINA!

Tom didn't do surprises. In all the years that they had been married, Rose had never known Tom to be spontaneous. She loved him to pieces, but predictability was one sure fact about her husband. It was, therefore, an amazing surprise when, last September at her birthday party, Tom had presented her with two air tickets for an African safari. They would leave the following March, flying to Kenya, and spend one week on safari and then one week at an East African beach resort on the coast of the Indian Ocean.

That had all been and gone, and already Rose was finding it difficult to recall the names of the other people on the safari. She picked up the photo album that Tom had put together of their trip and flipped through. As her eyes rested on the group photo of all six couples, she smiled to herself. Although it was a cliché, their holiday had truly been a holiday of a lifetime.

Right from the onset when they had arrived at Nairobi airport, having left Toronto in a blizzard, their eyes had never stopped blinking in amazement at the sights before them.

Africa had shocked their senses into overdrive. Everything was so different from Canada, and they had loved every bit of it.

The other five couples on the safari were introduced to Rose and Tom at the New Stanley Hotel, which was situated in the middle of the crazy busy city of Nairobi. There was Pete from Berkshire, England. He was a retired accountant from Reading and his petite wife Carol, was a retired nurse. The safari was a retirement present from their children.

Jan and Andre were from Windhoek in Southwest Africa. They had already been on several safaris, but all in South Africa. They were a little younger than Rose and Tom. Andre was a big bear of a man with thick, black curly hair and a beard. He had warm, friendly brown eyes that looked a bit like a Spaniel's. Jan, on the other hand, was quite petite and had fine, blonde hair cut into a bob and streaked with blonde highlights. She looked almost Nordic with her piercing blue eyes and high cheek bones and was very attractive wearing designer clothing, which Rose noticed straight away. They immediately struck up a friendship with each other vowing to stay in touch after the safari was over.

Doug and Polly were from Hampshire, England, and both were retired teachers. Doug had shocking white hair and awfully gappy teeth. He smoked like a chimney and was always cracking raucous jokes which Rose wasn't sure how to take, but he and Tom got along really well. His wife, Polly, barely said a word. She was pleasant enough and joined in with everything, but the word 'mousy' came to mind when Rose thought of her. Doug and Tom shared a beer together on more than one occasion and when Polly was asked if she would like to join them at the bar she always refused, making Rose feel awkward if she wanted to be with Tom. Doug and Tom shared the same sense of humour and spent most evenings laughing away at old jokes.

Then there was the young couple, Linda and John, who were on their honeymoon. They were so wrapped up with each other that they barely mingled with the rest of the group, going off to their beds long before anyone else. Rose smiled while remembering some of the sounds coming from within their tent.

The last couple, Baptiste and Juliette, were from Normandy in France and, although they spoke very good English, kept to themselves. Baptiste was a potter, and he looked a bit like an ancient hippie with long flowing shoulder length hair and irregular teeth that seemed to overcrowd his mouth. Juliette was a doctor and had worked for years with Médecins Sans Frontieres.

Whereas Baptiste was wild and free spirited, Juliette appeared to be the polar opposite. She was very tidily dressed in crisp, khaki shorts and pearly white cotton shirts and always wore a black head band to tie her long hair back off her face. They were not exactly unfriendly, but aloof was probably more the word to describe them. Rose had tried to hold a conversation with Juliette when she found out that she was a doctor with Médecins Sans Frontieres, Rose had been both impressed and interested to hear which countries she had worked in, but it seemed that Juliette did not want to talk about her work and had all but snubbed Rose.

Their orientation had taken place the day after their arrival and was conducted out on the hotel's terrace over-looking the swimming pool. They were to travel in two separate canvas topped Land Rovers. The first base camp was 12 km into the Masai Mara game reserve.

They had left Nairobi that same morning and had initially travelled on an impressive newly paved highway which soon gave way to a rutted, potholed dusty road with just a strip of tarmac in the middle. Rose remembered being jolted on the hard back seat of the Land Rover. Several times she had clung to Tom for fear of actually being bounced out of the open sided vehicle. The entrance to the game reserve had been exciting as a whole troop of baboons had camped by the wooden gates and, even though the driver had honked on his horn, the baboons had refused to leave their post until a bunch of bananas had been thrown to them. This, apparently, was such a regular occurrence that the drivers had taken to carrying bananas in their vehicles.

Rose remembered their first impression of the Masai Mara Lodge. The lodge was nestled in a clearing by the side of a small river. There were eight rondavels, little round huts with conical thatched roofs dotted all around the perimeter with one larger thatched building, in the middle. Stones painted white formed the edge to graveled pathways connecting the small cottages to the main lodge.

Everywhere Rose and Tom looked they could see a riot of colour, with lots of crimson red bougainvillea bushes as well as dahlias and zinnias of orange and gold, planted in flower beds around Frangipani trees, sweet in their fragrance and laden with waxy-white flowers growing from silver branches.

Around the perimeter of the lodge, majestic Jacaranda trees grew smothered in tiny bluebell-like flowers which formed a colourful blue carpet at the base of each tree. Honeysuckle tumbled over the entranceway to the lodge which, once inside, was all wooden panels and floors with floor to ceiling glass windows overlooking the slightly muddy looking river. Zebra and springbok skins were scattered over the floors. There were small round tables and chairs made from rattan and a bamboo bar.

Visitors to the lodge could watch the hippo's wallowing in

the mud by the side of the river, and if they waited long enough the odd crocodile would appear. Springboks, zebras, and lions regularly visited the river always with whole troops of baboons that seemed to have taken over the place. Their tour guide had warned them all never to feed any of the animals, particularly the baboons who had come to expect human food and were beginning to demand it.

Rose was a bit fearful of the baboons with their patchy, wiry short haired coats. She noticed that they all had very long, sharp yellowed teeth and fingernails, and their bright orange knobby bottoms looked suitably ugly. But it was their faces that perturbed Rose the most. Their clear, dark brown, shiny, beady, and intelligent eyes always looked cruel and calculating to Rose.

Their guides had also warned them about walking around in the dark. In Kenya daylight went from being light to dark almost instantly, like turning off a light switch. Leopards particularly liked to hunt at night and although the lodge had its own watchmen, sometimes a leopard had been known to creep into the fold and cause havoc, mostly with the chickens the cook kept for his kitchen. Rose and Tom had no intention of going anywhere at night although there was a night-time safari tour on offer, which they could take if they wanted.

Their rondavel huts were spotlessly clean with ceramic floors and whitewashed walls. They had their own toilet and wash basins inside, but all the showers were outside on a small, screened patio. The bedcovers and furniture were all white. A huge wooden bowl laden with tropical fruit sat on a small coffee table situated between two soft, white easy chairs. A vase of bright red cannon lilies sat on the dressing table next to a bottle of wine in an ice bucket with two wine glasses. On each pillow lay a silk pouch with Amarula liquor truffles nestled inside. The whole room was enchanting, and Rose loved it.

That first night at Masai Mara Lodge, Tom and Rose made love to the sounds of lions roaring and a whole cacophony of noises, as nocturnal animals padded past their window preparing to hunt for the night. Rose felt that she was on another planet - it was all so different and magical.

Another photograph in the album caught her attention. It was of Andre and Tom standing arm in arm with huge smiles on their faces. There was the watering hole in the background with a whole herd of elephants of all shapes and sizes in and out of the water. The whole memory of their elephant adventure came flooding back to Rose as if it was yesterday.

The "Night Safari' and the "Sunrise with Elephants" had been two of the extra packages included in the safari. Tom and Rose had opted for the elephant tour even though it had meant getting up at 4:00 a.m. Jan Du Preez had cried off claiming that she definitely was not a morning person and needed her beauty sleep.

They had all tumbled out of bed in the pitch darkness of night which had made Rose feel very nervous as in her mind those nocturnal leopards could still be out scavenging for the cook's chickens or worse. But Tom urged her to ignore all thoughts of big cats and soon they were safely aboard the open topped Land Rover and bumping along the rutted road. Daylight slowly crept in and the whole landscape was eerily bathed in grey and pink light.

The watering hole most commonly used by the reserve's herd of elephants was situated 30 kilometres from the lodge. The drive was magical as everything looked so different in the early morning light. Trees appeared like skeletons and there was something almost spooky about the mist rising from the ground in thin, whispery bands. It reminded Rose of a staged Halloween pageant. All they needed were a few witches and ghosts to appear to set the scene perfectly.

They arrived at the watering hole just as the sun rose. It was a truly spectacular site. The enormous red disc lined in purple streaks with pink, marshmallow clouds surrounding the whole sky.

The Land Rover driver parked under a giant baobab tree, and they all jumped out, although Tom helped Rose who was nervous about the jump down. Their guide beckoned for them to follow him. Once again Rose felt extremely apprehensive as there were shadows everywhere and strange noises pierced the night. She half expected a lion or leopard to leap out at the group at any moment.

The guide set up "camp" behind a large thorn bush and the first thing he did was warn the group to be on the lookout for snakes. The puff-adders were the worst as they were traditionally lazy and liked to bask in the sunshine. Many a traveler had accidentally stepped on these snakes and had not lived to tell the tale. It was not sunny yet, thought Rose, while carefully watching where she stepped. She did, however, wonder where those sun loving snakes slept at night.

The guide had chosen an excellent view of the muddy drinking hole for the elephants. The wait seemed like forever, but it was about twenty minutes before the first giant elephant appeared. He was a bull, one of the male elephants with tusks almost five feet in length. The guide explained that poachers still killed the elephants for their tusks, although Masai Mara Game Reserve had not had an incident of poaching for the past two years.

The grey shapes started moving towards the water like huge rocks in a steady stream. At first count Rose and Tom saw twelve fully grown elephants with three babies trailing along. How they didn't get trampled by the mammoth adults was beyond Rose.

Slowly, one by one, they filed down to the water where they proceeded to wade into the muddy water, then the fun began. It was like children playing at the seaside, trunks in the water, spraying each other playfully, swishing their trunks and tails, submerging their giant bodies, and coming up to a spray of water. They really did look as if they were enjoying themselves, even the babies joined in the fun.

There was one incident that frightened Rose and that was when two bull elephants started to butt each other aggressively with their giant tusks. It looked as if they were truly going to kill each other. The fight lasted all of five minutes, and it was difficult to tell who was victorious as both bulls walked away in opposite directions swinging their trunks, flapping their ears, and flicking their tails while shaking their whole head. *They were probably fighting over another female elephant,* Rose thought, *it was always about sex in the end.*

The tour concluded with a photo opportunity whereby the guide grouped everyone together with the elephants in the background. Rose then took a photo of just Tom and Andre standing arm in arm, looking so relaxed and happy that she was filled with a huge sense of gratitude. This rough, rugged African landscape appealed hugely to Tom. *He should have been born in Africa,* she thought, just like Andre.

Glancing at the photo album, again Rose smiled at the photograph of Tom, Andre, and Jan standing next to a cheetah cub called Uhuru. The cub had been found next to his mother who had been shot by a poacher.

Christopher, the Masai Lodge manager, had personally raised the young cub and now, at six months, he was as tame as any puppy dog and just as friendly. He would, in time, grow too big to handle and then they would start a program of rehabilitation, but until then, the guests at the lodge loved the opportunity to pet the young cub. In the photograph, Jan had her arms draped around 'Uhuru' while Andre, had his arms draped around her shoulders. Tom stood slightly to one side smiling at the camera. *They all looked so happy,* Rose thought.

With that last thought Rose closed the album and let out a big sigh. She glanced at her watch. It was ten o'clock, Tom would be back from pole-walking, and she would have to get her skates on if she was to bake the scones she had intended to bring around to her friend Susan Parker's house. She pulled out the ingredients, turned on the oven, and proceeded to make Susan's favourite orange and cranberry scones.

Susan. Every time Rose thought about her friend her heart gave a little lurch. She had gone through so much and her pain had been so palpable that Rose had not known how to help. The only thing that she could do was to be there for her, that and to cook.

When Susan was still living in London, Rose had driven over once or twice a week carrying casseroles and cakes, scones, and bottles of wine which they had both consumed over teary recollections of how life could have been with Henri Le Bruin had he not been killed in action the previous year. Susan and Henri were to be married having finally reconciled that one of them would have to move.

It had been Susan's decision to sell her darling cottage in London and move to Montreal where they would buy a home together. All those plans had changed in an instant on that one fateful day when Henri had been shot by Jim Reynolds at Centralia Airport.

Following the incident Susan had fallen into a massive depression, so much so that for months afterwards she had been unable to work, and last September she had finally handed in her notice.

After thirty years on the police force, Detective Inspector Susan Parker had retired, sold her house in London, and bought a condo in Harbour Court, Bayfield.

Now, almost nine months later, Rose's old friend was finally emerging from her cocoon-like state and had almost regained her previous 'joie de vivre.' She no longer looked gaunt and haggard. Her thick, chestnut coloured hair now glistened with health and renewed vitality, as did her eyes.

She had gained a bit of weight and had started dressing better. For the previous nine months Rose had only seen her friend wearing tatty t-shirts and jeans. The smart, elegant career woman had disappeared, only to be replaced with a lackluster, hollowed eyed shadow of the woman Rose had known. *Shock and trauma could do that to you,* Rose thought for the hundredth time, shock and grief at the loss of a loved one.

With the scones in the oven, Rose opened the back door and let Ben and Puff, her beloved dogs, outside. It was a beautiful day with not a single cloud in the turquoise blue sky. She could hear the birds singing. One particular song trilled out the loudest and Rose looked out to see where it was coming from. There, perched on one of the thin branches of the pear tree was a little red breasted robin singing its little heart out. Ben and Puff charged out into the garden and the small bird flew away. Rose decided to leave the dogs outside. Tom would be home within the hour, and it would be good for them to have some fresh air.

Rose gathered up the still warm scones and grabbed her car keys. She was about to leave when, on second thought, she stopped and found a scrap of paper to write a note for Tom telling him that she had gone to Susan's for coffee and that she would be back at lunch time. She had already told Tom her plans for the day, but he had been busy reading the newspaper and she wondered just how much he had taken in. Tom suffered from a form of 'deafness' called 'selective hearing' and it drove Rose crazy.

After lunch she had told Tom that she would go down to their boat, Tranquility, and give it a much needed clean. It had only been put back into the water a week and still had all the winter cobwebs and dust inside. Tom still had varnishing and some minor body work to complete, but the boating season had just begun.

Rose had just closed the front door and was about to jump in the car when she heard the telephone ring. Quickly opening the door and retracing her steps back to the kitchen, she grabbed the phone. There was total silence on the other end and then the broken ring tone as the phone was disconnected.

Someone had obviously dialed the wrong number, Rose thought as she once more walked out to the car and prepared to visit Susan, her friend.

ABOUT THE AUTHOR

Over the past thirty years Judy has written twenty novellas, various collections of poetry and a number of plays. Judy wrote her first full length novel in 2013 and developed it into a series called the Rose Blair Murder Mysteries all set in the sleepy village of Bayfield on the beautiful shores of Lake Huron in Ontario, Canada.

Judy and her husband reside in Bayfield with their beloved dog Susie and cat Thomas and enjoy visits from their children and grandchildren.

After retiring Judy and her husband took on a new challenge in their lives. Purchasing land on the outskirts of Bayfield they have planted a six-acre vineyard and are in the process of designing and building a boutique winery.

Life is beautiful and sweet. I feel so very blessed with all my wonderful family and friends who continually surround me with their love.